SHOT IN THE DARK

It was close to midnight when Will heard the hoof beats of moving horses. Presently he could make out the dim form of a rider approaching the corral gate. Silently Will pushed the door open and stepped out into the night, lifting his gun from its holster. He moved swiftly toward the dismounted man and then called sharply, "Hold on there!"

As he spoke an orange flare and the racketing shot of a pistol boomed out from his left. Will half turned and shot blindly at the flame, knowing as he did so that he should not have returned the fire but should have dropped to the ground.

And then the big sound came and a tearing agony slammed at his back and side, knocking him flat on his face in the dirt of the corral. He knew then that he'd walked into a trap. In those terrible seconds he was certain he was going to die, drowning in an ocean of pain. . . .

Books by Luke Short

THE WHIP

LUKE SHORT

A DELL BOOK

Published by
Dell Publishing
a division of
Bantam Doubleday Dell Publishing Group, Inc.
666 Fifth Avenue
New York, New York 10103

ISBN: 0-440-20961-7

Reprinted by arrangement with the Frederick D. Glidden Estate

Printed in the United States of America

Published simultaneously in Canada

April 1992

10 9 8 7 6 5 4 3 2 1

OPM

THE WHIP

1

Will Gannon sat with his back against the log wall and watched the stage driver get drunk. Outside, the March blizzard they had bucked through the afternoon was tearing at the eaves of the stage station, but he thought it might be diminishing. Before him, his tin plate of food marbled with cold grease lay untouched; he leaned against the wall with a relaxed numbness, long legs stretched under the trestle table, and watched his dazed fellow passengers blot up the warmth of this smoky low-ceilinged room.

Across the lamplit room at the point farthest from the plank bar where the stage driver was drinking, Bates Boley's daughter was serving up the last of the past-midnight suppers. She was a pretty, sullen-faced girl whose slatternly dress and unbrushed hair seemed a kind of protective coloration against the drab filth of the unfloored room.

Empty-handed now, she was heading back for the kitchen when she spied Gannon's plate. Halting beside him, close enough so that she purposely touched him, she asked, "Not hungry?"

"I'm hungry, but not that hungry."

He looked up at her, his green eyes chill under heavy black brows. They expressed the sum of his temper which, on the ninth day out from Carson

City, was a little raveled with impatience and unnecessary discomfort.

The girl seemed to take no offense. "You try it sometime when you got nothing but bear to cook up."

"I have. I've done a better job with the hide alone."

Surprisingly, she giggled. Ignoring her, Will lifted the half-filled cup of pale whiskey which he had diluted to drinkable proportions at the water bucket by the door. Drinking, he watched the stage driver, his buffalo coat open, prop himself securely in the wedge of bar and wall and disdainfully contemplate the passengers he soon would be carrying. Less than a half-hour before, the bottle before him was full. It was two-thirds empty now and Gannon, remembering from four years back what lay east of the Rock Creek Station, felt a slow anger stir within him.

Beside Gannon the express messenger, a small, red-faced, hard-bitten man still wearing his buffalo coat, was eating the wretched food and occasionally glancing at the driver. Now, at the foot of the table a grim-lipped man past middle age rose, put his hand on the shoulder of an exhausted-looking boy who was shaking almost uncontrollably as the heat of the room thawed him, and skirted the bench to approach the messenger.

"You been watching the new driver?" the man demanded.

"I have, Mr. Dickert," the messenger replied, his tone barely polite.

"He's got close to a bottle in him," Dickert said in a tone of outrage.

The messenger shrugged.

"He'll never make the stage, let alone drive it!" the older man said angrily. Now he looked at Gannon for confirmation, but Gannon said nothing.

"His business," the messenger said.

"I won't ride with him and I won't lay over in this sty," Dickert said angrily. "I want you to do something."

Now the messenger looked squarely at him. "You find us another driver and we'll talk," he said flatly, adding, "The best thing to do is eat up and get out of here before he drinks any more."

The older man wheeled away and returned to his bench, his back stiff with anger. The messenger looked fleetingly at Gannon, shrugged, and returned to his food. Reluctantly, Gannon came to the decision he had been considering.

Slowly he rose and rounded the table, heading for the bar. He was a tall man, made taller by thick black grey-shot hair parted deeply on the side, and only the closest observer would have detected the slight limp in his stride. He was wearing a corduroy coat and a rough-knit, neck-high sweater, and his long face, not lately shaved, held a reserve bordering on taciturnity.

The driver, a burly man wearing a spade beard chopped off at the first button on his shirt, was propped against the bar. His whip and buckskin gloves lay on the plank beside the almost empty bottle of whiskey. He was leisurely fumbling with the buttons on his buffalo coat when Gannon halted in front of him.

"Still trying to drink it all, Harvey?"

The driver stared at him in Olympian drunkenness, and then recognition came. He straightened a little and said thickly, "No affair of yours any more, Gannon."

"I thought I'd blacklisted you."

"You run your Carson division and let Maydet run his." He groped for his gloves and whip, found them, and straightened up.

"You know which door you're going through?" Gannon asked softly.

The driver looked first at the outside door, then at the door which led to the bunk room, and then returned his glance to the outside door. Lifting his whip majestically, he pointed to it and said, "That one."

Slowly Gannon fisted his hand, extended his thumb, and lifted his fist over his right shoulder. "No. That one. You'll sleep it off."

"Stand away," the driver said disdainfully and pushed away from the wall, raising his left arm to brush Gannon aside. Will simply pivoted under the arm and sank his left fist into the driver's exposed midriff. As the man's head came away from the wall in an unconscious jackknife of his body, Gannon looped a savage blow to his bearded jaw. The driver's head rapped back against the wall and slowly he slipped down to a sitting position. Then, all balance gone, he rolled over on his side.

At that moment Bates Boley entered from the night and slammed the plank door behind him. His ragged coat and battered hat were powdered with snow; tiny icicles clung to his matted mustache and beard. Leaning against the door, while he furiously dry-washed his hands to warm them, he called, "Ready to go, folks," and only then noticed the prone driver.

There was utter silence in the room as Gannon picked up the driver's whip and gauntlets and tramped back toward the bench which held his buffalo coat and black hat. He had almost reached his coat before the first passenger spoke. "How do we get out of here?"

Will halted and looked over the dozen passengers. Some were already muffled to the ears in coats and scarfs. He read shock, dismay, and anger in their faces.

"I'll drive," he announced flatly.

Now Mr. Dickert rose from beside the boy and came up to Gannon. "You ever drive a stage before?"

"Two years on Butterfield, a year on Midland. Until last week I was Midland's division agent at Carson City."

Bates Boley found his voice now. "You a company man?"

Gannon looked at him coldly. "Not any more. If I was, you'd be out of a job."

Now Gannon turned his head to look at the express messenger, flat challenge in his green eyes. But the messenger, still seated, said in a noncommittal voice, "I've heard of you."

"Then we'll be going, gentlemen." He tossed his dollar for whiskey and his untouched supper upon the table, shrugged into his heavy coat, and, indifferent to the indecision reflected on the faces of the passengers, crossed the room, opened the door, and stepped out into the night. Outside the wind pushed against him and the lantern which he took from a nail on the log wall guttered wildly. Tramping through the half-foot of snow, he circled the teams, who were losing their heavy winter coats; their rumps were already silver with snow. Bates Boley scurried ahead of him and was holding the reins of the six teams when Gannon approached and handed him the lantern. Gannon stood silently watching the express messenger count his fares as they filed into the curtained coach. Finished, the messenger climbed into the box and only then did Gannon step up beside him.

Boley handed up the reins, saying sourly, "I hope you know what you're doing. Just remember I didn't like it."

"That will be filed with the general superintendent," Gannon said drily. He shook out his whip, kicked off the brake, and shouted his teams into motion, headed for the break in the black timber that was the stage route east. The timber gave some protection from the wind and the stage was strangely soundless except for the creaking and for the cheerful harness jangle. Gannon drove effortlessly once he had taken the measure of the lead team, trusting them because they knew the road. He had only to sense the places to brake and keep the swing team working.

Once the quality of the new driver was proven, the express messenger relaxed and tried to engage Gannon in conversation. Will's laconic replies, however, discouraged him, and Will's thoughts returned to the events in Boley's station. Perhaps he shouldn't have hit Harvey but it seemed to him that force had been necessary. A year ago he had dismissed Harvey from his division for overturning a messenger coach while dead drunk, and had followed company regulations by blacklisting him.

Now Harvey had turned up on Midland's Louisburg division.

The incident, he thought, only underlined what he had learned from a hundred passengers he had quizzed: west of Salt Lake the Midland had a reputation for being the finest stage line in America; east of it the line was the worst in the West. Report had it that the schedule was a consistent shambles and sixty days' mail was backed up. Indians and white riffraff preyed on the line, and added to this was the enormously difficult terrain with its mountain passage.

Within an hour they had descended out of the deep fresh snow, reaching the belt where the thaws and freezes of late spring had dropped great boulders on the mud-slick, slushy road. A dozen times in the next few hours, Gannon had to rein in and call for help to move a boulder off the narrow road and send it crashing into the far stream below.

Before daylight they were out of the snow but not out of the timber. They changed teams at a swing station where the stocktender worked by lantern light, and afterwards, as dawn broke, Gannon saw they were into the drab, bare, foothill country. At full daylight the Concord came to a halt beside the single log building joined by a barn and empty corral that was the next swing station.

The moment the stage came to a halt Gannon knew something was wrong. The corral was empty, in itself a warning, and the building dark, yet the door was open. Reaching down on the boot, he brought up a rifle and only then did the express messenger beside him come alive.

"Where's Keefe?"

Gannon swung down, not bothering to answer. He tramped across the hard-packed dirt, heading for the open door, his rifle ready. Suddenly he halted and turned his head sideways, listening. He picked up the sound now; it was that of a man running and it came from behind the log shack.

Then, rounding the corner of the adobe at a dead run, rifle in hand, came the hatless figure of a young man. At sight of Gannon and the express messenger now standing beside him, he hauled up, chest heaving. He might have been nineteen, but the anger in his thin-lipped, tense face was mature enough, Will saw.

"I'm new," Gannon said. "Isn't this our swing station?"

"It was up to this morning," the stocktender said bitterly. "I don't know what the hell it is now."

"What's wrong, Keefe?" the express messenger asked.

"You see any horses here? You see anything that looks like a team change?"

No answer was necessary and now the young man tiredly knelt on one knee and scrubbed his sweating face with his sleeve. "They hit me like this two, three times a year."

"Indians?"

The stocktender eyed him bitterly. "Indians, hell."

A couple of the passengers approached now and the stocktender went on. "The division won't send me feed, so I've got to try and loose-herd the horses while they graze, and still watch the station. Yesterday the westbound was late. Before I could change teams for it and round up the stock, it was dark. This morning I aimed to turn out early and round them up before you got here. They beat me to it."

"Who's they?" Will asked.

The stocktender swore. "Breeds, Snakes, Sioux, Cheyennes, hardcases, and for all I know, Sunday School teachers. All I know is they're horse thieves."

Gannon felt a sudden pity for the stocktender. For forty dollars a month, paid quarterly, he lived a solitary, dangerous existence under the moral obligation to keep his bit of stage line functioning. He was at the mercy of any passing band of Indians, of whatever tribe, and this plains area and the mountains behind it housed half the riffraff of the West. Now the stocktender rose, eyeing Gannon's teams. He totally ignored the passengers as he said, "You got twelve miles to Lennor's with a long stretch of blow sand." He looked at the messenger. "Pass the word on to Maydet that I'll stick until he gets somebody to take this over."

"Maydet?" Will asked.

"Division superintendent at Louisburg. He better get someone in a week, or I'll throw the key in the water bucket and ride out."

"On what?" Will asked.

The stocktender suddenly grinned. "All right, walk out."

Gannon turned then to regard his teams. The deep snow, the cold, and the uncertain footing had left them tired, but since there was no relief they must be used. Summoning the passengers, he and the express messenger climbed into the box and he whipped the reluctant teams into motion. He had only another hour of grass before they hit stretches of blow sand on the level prairie.

To spare his weary horses, Gannon ordered all passengers to walk. In the worst spots he directed his passengers to push the stage through the axle-deep sand. Once when they were totally bogged, both teams and passengers exhausted from their efforts to move the stage, an immigrant train consisting of four ox teams and wagons slowly hove over the prairie horizon. It took them an hour to reach the stage, but only minutes to hook up the oxen to the stage and free it.

By noon the monotony of the prairie combined with the exertion of the morning had put the messenger to sleep. Off to the south was the continuous line of grey that marked the leafless cottonwoods on the river bottom. Patiently Gannon nursed his exhausted teams along and presently, past the middle of this grey day, he saw the buildings ahead that marked Lennor's station.

Approaching it, he regarded the trim white-painted frame house with a kind of surprised recollection. In a country where even logs had to be freighted, this house was built of milled lumber, hauled from a mill far to the east. The log barns were trim, and the corrals of cedar posts stout and straight. As the stage hauled up before the long veranda, Gannon set the brakes, threw down the reins to the stocktender, and stiffly descended. Lennor's home station, he supposed, would be elected as a lay-over for a good half of the weary passengers.

A stern-faced, grey-haired man in rough work clothes greeted the passengers as they descended, while a stocktender began to unhook the teams. Will waited until the passengers filed into the house and then mounted the steps to the porch where the sober-faced man was waiting.

"You're new," the man said. "I'm Lennor. Where's Cummings?"

"At Boley's. Too drunk to drive," Gannon said drily.

Lennor shook his head. "I didn't think that was possible," he said sourly. He looked at Gannon with mild curiosity, as if wondering how a stage driver could materialize at Boley's. Will knew, however, that this was no concern of Lennor's and he brushed past him and stepped inside. The big common room was a pleasant place, its puncheon floor holding a long table with benches, a big barreled stove, and dark walnut furniture that Will knew had been freighted from the East. In one corner under the stairs rising to the second story, he saw a neat stack of more than a dozen bulging mail sacks and canvas sacks that carried public documents.

The passengers were seating themselves at the long table and Will took a corner place on the bench with his back to the kitchen. A plain, grey-haired woman whom Gannon took to be Lennor's wife began serving up coffee while the passengers loaded their plates from the platters of elk steaks and piping hot biscuits. Gannon helped himself and was eating hungrily when a slim arm holding a big coffee pot reached over his shoulder and filled his pint cup.

"You're the new driver," a pleasant voice said.

Gannon looked around and saw a girl standing behind him, a beginning smile on her face. She was slim and could have been twenty, and the first thing Will noticed about her were her eyebrows winging thick and dark over pale green eyes. A mass of shiny chestnut hair was brushed cleanly away from her temples and was gathered by a ribbon at the base of her neck. Her grey dress, Will noted, was darned and patched but spotlessly clean, and there was a faint dusting of freckles across the bridge of her small nose. Her lips were full and, as her smile faded under Will's cool appraisal, they set in a sober self-assurance.

"Emergency only," Will said.

Now the girl came around the corner of the table so that Will did not have to crane his neck to see her. He supposed she was Lennor's daughter. She asked matter-of-factly, "Did Mrs. Soderstrom give you garden seed for me?"

"I don't know any Mrs. Soderstrom, and I have no garden seed," Will said. "Was I supposed to have some?"

"Cummings said he'd remind her."

"Try another driver," Will said drily. "Still I doubt if you'll have any better luck."

The girl frowned. "Why do you say that?"

Fork in hand, Will pointed with it to the sacks of mail under the stairs in the corner of the room. "If they can't remember to pick up mail sacks, they can't remember to pick up your garden seed."

Color came into the girl's face. "We show every westbound driver the sacks."

"Quit feeding them until they move them."

The girl looked at him levelly and then said quietly, "Why don't you tell that to the division agent instead of scolding innocent people?"

"Why don't I?" Will murmured, complete indifference in the tone of his voice. He returned to his food, thinking that the girl was right. Still the drivers in this division were apparently more concerned about running errands for the station women than they were about moving U.S. mail. But it was no concern of his now, he thought. Once he had delivered his coach at Louisburg, the end of the division, he was through with staging. Midland's affairs were no concern of his.

Finished, he rose and went out onto the veranda, leisurely packing his pipe.

Across the road a stocktender was greasing the axles while a second man was driving out the team change. Back of the coach a pair of dismounted riders were talking to Lennor. One of them, a tall burly man dressed in a ragged pony coat that fell below his knees, picked up Gannon's exit and was watching him with a veiled alertness. His full face was not lately shaven, yet Gannon could see the knife scar that ran from the corner of his full-lipped mouth to his jaw hinge. A semicircle of black mustache gave him an oddly oriental look that was accentuated by his black, arrogant eyes. His companion, dressed in a cast-off Army overcoat under which was a holstered pistol, lazily leaned against the coach; he was watching Gannon too.

Lennor said something to the big man, then looked at Gannon, and all three men moved away from the saddle horse, toward the veranda. Gannon put his shoulder against the pillar of the veranda and regarded them idly as they came up to him and halted.

The big man said, "What happened to Cummings?"

Gannon looked at him, getting the vague impression that the man's voice held some authority.

"He was drunk."

"How drunk?"

"About a bottle drunk."

The big man turned and said to his companion, "Hear that, Rich?"

Richie Cleff had derisive dark eyes that burned like a banked fire, promising total wildness when anger came. His lean, unshaven face held a dormant viciousness and now he observed jeeringly, "Who would that worry?"

"Me," Gannon said quietly.

The big man said then, "You drove, Lennor tells me. Couldn't Cummings make the box?"

"Not after I hit him."

The big man's mouth slacked sideways in a sour smile, but there was no humor in his eyes. "So you drove."

Gannon nodded.

The big man held out his hand. "I'll take your ticket. You've gone as far as you'll go on Midland."

Gannon straightened up. "Who's talking?"

"Lou Maydet, division agent."

"You want some rules quoted at you?" Gannon asked mildly.

"No."

"You can take up a ticket, but you can't take up a pass."

Maydet's expression altered. "You with the line?"

Gannon tilted his head in the affirmative and now Maydet looked down at Cleff, as if for guidance.

"Prove it," Cleff said gently.

"Not to you," Will said.

He saw a swift flick of anger in Cleff's eyes and then the smaller man said softly, "Don't get tough, friend. You don't look twelve feet tall to me."

Gannon lazily regarded him, then looked at Maydet. "He work for you?"

Maydet nodded and then said mildly, "Quit it, Rich."

His glance shuttled back to Gannon. Obviously he was troubled. The fact that Gannon had hit one of his drivers, brought the stage through himself, and casually refused to be intimidated, impressed him. Gannon knew he was wondering what company rank this stranger held and if it was wise to annoy him further. Gannon decided to remain on the offensive, and he said, "Your first swing station west was raided last night. The stocktender said if you haven't replaced him in a week he'll be gone."

Maydet scowled. "Keefe? What happened?"

"They cleaned him out, down to his saddle horse even."

Maydet swore and looked fleetingly at his companion, who had not removed his gaze from Gannon's face.

Now Gannon straightened up, knocked out his pipe, and said, "You got a driver to take my place?"

Apparently the fact had not occurred to the division agent that he had not only tried to force his driver off the stage but that it was his responsibility to supply a replacement. He scowled in concentration and Gannon was watching him when he heard footsteps behind him. He turned and saw the girl halted, looking at him. There was mischief in her green eyes, but she said unsmilingly, "There's your man. Complain to him."

Will felt a swift irritation. The girl had refused to take his mild bullyragging and had neatly turned the tables on him. He saw Maydet look from the girl to him.

"What complaint?" Maydet asked.

"Why don't you move your mail?" Will asked quietly.

"Why do you care?" Richie Cleff asked instantly.

"I don't," Will said mildly. "I'm just curious. Midland's mail contract with the government is what feeds you. Keep this up and the government will cancel."

"So you're worrying about us?" Cleff asked softly.

Will looked at him. "Not any."

Cleff said thinly, "You've got a long nose, friend."

"I have at that," Will conceded, indifference again in his voice, as he looked at the girl.

Passengers began to file out and Maydet touched Cleff's arm. When Cleff reluctantly shuttled his gaze from Will to Maydet, the division agent nodded his head toward the coach. Slowly, with a sidelong look at Will, Cleff turned and both men moved across the road. Now Will looked at the girl.

"I didn't think you'd do it," the girl said.

Will pushed away from the veranda post and pocketed his pipe. "That squares us. I didn't think you would either." He touched his hat and went down the steps, tramping toward the coach. He nodded good-bye to Lennor, who said, "That was none of my doing. I tried to tell him you'd done the line a favor."

Will didn't even halt. He said, "It doesn't matter," and moved toward the coach.

Richie Cleff was in the box, Gannon noted, along-side the express messenger, and Maydet sat on the top seat behind them. *Why, he's going east,* Gannon thought with surprise. The next station west was without teams and without feed, its horses stolen, and yet Maydet was not bothering about it.

Four of the passengers had elected to stay over, so that Gannon had a seat inside. He had barely pulled his coat around him before he was sleeping.

It was evening of the next day when the stage pulled into Louisburg. This was the closest thing to a town since Salt Lake, yet it held only a handful of log buildings. The largest, a two-story affair, was the hotel, across the road from a long log building, a combination store and saloon at which the stage pulled up. Ahead were the blacksmith shops, sta-bles, and corrals. A couple of bulky warehouses flanked the dim-lit hotel and there was a tangle of freight and immigrant wagons beyond the store. Louisburg, Gannon remembered as he stepped out of the stage, was not only a home station on the Midland, but a terminus of other stage lines to the east and south. He had heard embittered travelers tell of days spent in this wretched collection of hov-els awaiting passage west on the Midland. Miners, anxious to reach the gold fields in the north, would even pool together and hire a special stage in order to avoid waiting their turn for the west in Louisburg.

Gannon stretched his travel-stiffened legs and looked about him. Maydet rode the stage on to the stables where the teams ended their chore. Gannon fell away from the other passengers, who were head-ing for the hotel and turned toward the lamplit saloon. A pair of Cavalry troopers, drunk and quietly quarreling, were on the single step, and Gannon skirted them and moved inside. The low-ceilinged room was smoke-filled and the rough bar to the left ran its length. A score of men—immigrants, escort troops, miners for the west, and dusty travelers—lined the bar. A half-dozen men stood around the faro table at the rear and a large poker game was in progress at the round front table.

Gannon came up to the bar, ordered whiskey, and then tiredly scrubbed his face with the palm of his hand.

He was aware of a man coming up to the bar beside him, but he paid no attention until he heard the man say, "Smelled any 'Paches lately?"

From the dim recesses of memory Gannon identified the phrase and he turned. His poker hand still in his grimy fist, an unshaven, roughly dressed young man stood waiting, a smile on his face. Slowly Gannon extended his hand, smiling, too.

"Hutch!" he said warmly, and they shook hands. "You're a long ways from Arizona."

"Not far enough, Will. How've you been?"

The two men regarded each other with open affection. Hutch Forney had been a Butterfield driver when Gannon had worked for the Southern Line. They had helped in the grueling task of keeping that desert route open; they had shared a hundred camp fires and as many bottles of whiskey. Hutch, Gannon knew, was the born improvident—happy-go-lucky, always generous, totally reckless, and blindly loyal. He had been wild and fiddle-footed and in his cheerful lean face Gannon saw no indication that he had changed. When the Butterfield Line was closed down and its equipment moved to the north, Gannon had come north. Hutch had drifted to Tucson and out of Will's life, leaving only the pleasant memory of a man irrepressibly gay in spirit.

"Heard you've got a Nevada division," Hutch said.

"Where'd you hear that?"

"Oh, I work for the line, too." Hutch grimaced. "I've got the Helper Creek Station West. A real lonesome place, even with a wife. I get to come in once in a while and look at myself in the bottom of a glass."

"Wife?" Gannon said drily. "That could mean children."

Hutch laughed. "One. Half Papago, half Irish, and born with a sunburn." A kind of defiance lay behind the laughter in Hutch's eyes, and Gannon knew the story. Papagos were Arizona Indians and in that womanless country Hutch had probably picked up with a pretty Indian girl. Too loyal to desert her and too restless to stay put, Hutch had probably brought her into this alien and hard land where he would sire half-breed children who would be totally rootless. Hutch was more than a squaw man, Gannon thought; he had forfeited the society of his own kind, yet he had not even acquired the society of his wife's kind. For a fleeting moment Gannon felt pity for him.

"You a family man?" Hutch asked. Gannon did not answer: he signaled the bartender for drinks.

"Hutch, come along," one of the poker players called.

Hutch turned. "Raise it five," he called back. Then, his body shielding his cards from the players,

he spread his hand on the bar and looked up at Will.
He was, Will saw, trying to fill an inside straight.

Gannon shook his head. "I'm afraid you'll never
own a bank."

Hutch lifted his glass of whiskey, nodded to Will,
and tossed off his drink. Carefully he wiped his
mouth with the back of his hand, then said, "Remember me? When you run out of luck just come to
old Hutch. He's got more than he can use."

He grinned, picked up his hand and turned. "You
be around?" At Gannon's nod, Hutch winked and
went back to his game.

Will downed his drink, suddenly hungry, and
pushed away from the bar. As he passed the poker
game, he saw Hutch raking in the pot and on his
face was the happy expression of a man who was
living only for the moment.

Gannon stepped out into the night and crossed
the road toward the hotel and there was a sadness in
him. He was glad that he had been sleeping through
the team change at Helper Creek so that he had
been spared the sight of Hutch's home and family.
He could imagine its cheerless squalor that Hutch
even now was trying to escape.

Mounting the steps of the hotel, Gannon entered
the bare and dirty lobby. The dining room was on
the left, and for a moment, noting the silence, he
wondered if it had closed for the night. Throwing his
coat over one of the lobby chairs, he stepped into
the dining room and saw that there were still several
men eating. Two long tables filled the room and as
Will moved toward one of the tables his glance
touched a lone diner seated with his back to the
door. For a brief moment the set of the man's back,

the bristling shock of close-cropped grey hair was familiar, and then he halted. A fleeting annoyance touched him and he felt the impulse to turn and retreat, and then resignation came to him and he moved on toward the man.

Halting behind the grey-haired man, Gannon said quietly, "How are you, Mr. Olderson?"

The man looked up and for a moment there was disbelief in his square face. Then the smile came and he rose, holding out his hand. "Will! Have I got the wrong station and the wrong town?"

Gannon smiled. "No. Still, I can't blame you for wondering."

Olderson gestured toward the bench and they both sat down. Now Olderson pushed his plate away and regarded Gannon with a touch of curiosity showing in his face. Will knew that Olderson had not achieved the general superintendency of Midland by being polite and he knew that the older man was shocked, disturbed, and curious.

"I'm sort of off the reservation," Gannon said.

"Twelve hundred miles or so," Olderson said pleasantly. "Any trouble come up, Will?"

"I quit. I wrote you a letter a week for three months."

"I didn't get them."

"I can understand that, after seeing the way the mail's backed up in this division."

Olderson grimaced. "True enough."

"I didn't want to wait any longer, so I took off."

The older man looked carefully at Will. "Haven't we treated you right, Will?"

Gannon nodded his black head. "You know you have."

"Then what's the trouble?"

Gannon's face hardened, but he hesitated only a bare moment. "Nothing to do with you or the line, Mr. Olderson."

The older man looked steadily at him. "I think I have the right to know."

"So you do," Gannon said after a pause. He took a deep breath and said tonelessly, "Marian left me. She decided she'd rather live with a San Francisco shipowner than be a stage line division agent's wife."

Both pain and sympathy were reflected in Olderson's eyes. There was embarrassment, too, and he looked down at his plate. Then he said, "I'm sorry to hear that, Will. I'd thought that marriage was one that would stay."

Now he looked up at Gannon, who acknowledged his words with a bleak silence.

A look of understanding came into Olderson's face. "A change of scenery, is that it?"

"Something like that."

"What will you do?"

"I've been shot up once and discharged. Maybe they'll have me back."

At the same moment they both became aware of a young man approaching their table. Gannon recognized him as the companion of Mr. Dickert, who had challenged him at Boley's station.

The lad halted at the table and said to Olderson, "You sent for me, sir?"

Olderson looked at him blankly. "I don't recollect doing so, my boy."

"You're Mr. Olderson?"

The older man nodded, and now a look of puzzlement came into the boy's face. "I was in our room when a man knocked on the door and said you wanted to see me."

Olderson looked at Will, who said to the boy, "When was this?"

"Just now."

Will rose, asking, "Which room is yours?"

"Five."

Without a word Will went across the dining room, premonition pushing him. Turning left, he took the stairs two at a time and when he reached the second floor he had drawn his pistol. Halfway down the dim-lit corridor he saw that room No. 5 would be the rear room.

Olderson and the boy achieved the second story as Will halted before the closed door of room No. 5. He did not even raise his hand to knock, but palmed open the door.

On the floor lay Mr. Dickert. He was sprawled on his back and the whole of his shirt front was soggy with shiny blood. He had, Will saw, been expertly knifed, probably as he opened the door. His shirttail was out and the waist band of his trousers had been cut. At a glance Will knew that the murderer, in his haste to get Dickert's money belt before young Dickert could reappear, had slashed the belt.

Will's glance lifted to the open window and he moved around Dickert's body toward it, hearing Olderson's footsteps in the corridor. Leaning out the window, Gannon saw the roof of the kitchen shed some four feet below the window.

Now he turned and saw Olderson and young Dickert standing just within the room. For a moment Gannon thought the boy would faint; his face

drained of blood and he closed his eyes. Will moved
swiftly toward him, put an arm around his shoulder,
turned him and moved him out into the corridor,
then gently propped him against the wall.

"Is—is he dead?" the boy asked in a whisper.

"I'm afraid so," Gannon said.

Olderson came out of the room, and when Will
looked at him he saw the smouldering rage in the
older man's eyes. Olderson said gently, "I'm sorry,
lad. You were decoyed out of the room so that this
man could be murdered and robbed. Was he your
father?"

"My uncle," the boy whispered.

"And was he carrying a sum of money in a money
belt?"

The boy only nodded.

Olderson sighed. "Come," he said. Gently he led
the boy down the hall, opened the door to his own
room, and gestured toward the chair, at the same
time turning to Will. "Will you have them send up
some whiskey, Will? I think it would help him. I'll
stay."

Before he left the room Will saw the boy slack
into the chair and bury his face in his hands. Downstairs Will told the desk clerk what had happened,
and the clerk vanished into the kitchen.

Will stood irresolute in the middle of the lobby,
feeling a helpless rage. A man had just been savagely murdered, yet what was there to do about it?
With the town full of strangers, who would hunt
down the killer, since there was no law officer to
receive the report of the murder? Beyond that, who
in this whole town would concern himself with the
death of a total stranger? No one would miss the

dead man except a bewildered and helpless boy. *He'll grow up quick,* Gannon thought wryly.

The clerk hurried up the stairs with the whiskey and now Will realized that he had not eaten the meal he had come here for. Going into the dining room, he asked for his supper, which was served by a surly man in a soiled apron. As he ate, he pondered the older Dickert's murder and the circumstances surrounding it. When he was finishing his coffee, Olderson came into the dining room and sat down on the bench.

"I think the whiskey knocked him out," Olderson said grimly, then added, "It's shameful, shameful! This filthy shantytown should be burned to the ground."

"Including your office and stages, Mr. Olderson?"

The older man looked sharply at him. "What do you mean by that?"

"That murder was planned on your stage line."

Olderson was silent a moment, watching him. "How do you figure so?"

"Young Dickert was asked for by name. Who'd know his name unless they saw the passenger list? No man planning murder is fool enough to leave a trail by asking to see a hotel register."

Olderson was watching but he kept silent as Gannon went on, "Why was murder necessary? A stranger could have stuck a gun in Dickert's belly, demanded his money, and left. He didn't though. Which proves Dickert had seen this man, so Dickert had to be killed."

Olderson was still silent, weighing Gannon's words. "A passenger, you think?"

Gannon only shrugged. "Passengers or not, I'd

guess there were two of them. One had to be a stranger to ask for young Dickert by name and tell him to go find you. The boy would have recognized a passenger, but he didn't recognize this man. Afterwards a man the older Dickert knew murdered him for his money." He paused. "It was all planned on your stage line."

Olderson looked down at his stubby hands clasped before him and nodded. "The guilt doesn't end there, Will. Maydet is our division superintendent. This is his town. Nothing happens here that he or his crew don't know of." He paused and then said wryly, "We're back in the Middle Ages, when we murder and rob any traveler who can't defend himself."

Gannon nodded, sharing some of Olderson's righteous wrath. He watched the older man draw a black cigar from his breast pocket, examine it, and then stick it in his mouth, making no attempt to light it.

Abruptly Olderson looked at him and asked quietly, "Have you run far enough, Will?"

Will looked at him, puzzled as to his meaning.

"Have you run far enough?" Olderson repeated. "A man can always try to run from things he doesn't like to remember, but I've never heard of it working out. Have you run far enough?"

Will felt the color coming into his face and he said stiffly, "That would be my business, wouldn't it?"

"No. It's mine," Olderson said, almost roughly. "If you've run far enough, stay here. I need you. I need a new division superintendent to replace Maydet. Mail is backed up sixty days. What stock hasn't been stolen is half starved. Most of our own stations serve garbage, and we have no schedule. After tonight, it seems that we don't stop at murder."

Listening to him, considering what he said, Will thought of what lay ahead of him. Olderson was right; he was running from something, but that something was in his mind and always would be, wherever he ran. A man must do something, and this offer of Olderson's was more than a job; it was an expression of Olderson's deep confidence in him. If he had failed with a wife, did it mean that he would fail with a job? Was that part of what he was running from?

Olderson interrupted his thoughts. "Think it over, Will."

"You've done my thinking for me," Will said wryly. "I'll take it."

2

At six next morning Gannon and Olderson stepped out onto the sagging porch of the hotel and went down the steps, heading for Maydet's big log general store which also housed the stage station. It was a grey chill day and the wind against Gannon's freshly shaven cheek had a bite in it from the new snow in the mountains.

Olderson tramped purposefully behind a freshly lighted cigar which was pointed at a stage making up in front of the store.

Gannon, in last night's darkness, had missed the scattering of drab log shacks which at times were completely hidden by sheets of dust picked up by the spring wind. Miners and waiting travelers aimlessly crossed and recrossed the wide road, waiting for the stages that would move them out.

Olderson stepped around a couple of breeds wrapped in their blankets squatting by the doorway and entered the low-ceilinged general store. To the left was a boarded-up section with a counter, which was the post office. The long counter extended toward the back of the store and a half-dozen loafers were seated on it. There was a matching counter on the right, and against the window was a small enclosure behind a crude railing. This was the stage office.

Maydet, still unshaven, his black hair uncombed,

sat sidewise in a swivel chair beside a roll-top desk, two fingers of each hand jammed in the lower pockets of a greasy buckskin vest, his booted feet resting among a mass of papers atop the desk. Cleff, wearing the tattered Army overcoat, lounged on the rail, his back to the door. Maydet was giving orders to two roughly dressed men standing inside the enclosure. Gannon observed this crew with a rising distaste and then glanced about the low-ceilinged store. Goods of all kinds were piled helter-skelter on the counters and in the corners, and even hung from the ceiling. A trio of unshaven clerks who seemed indifferent to this disorder went about their slow business of waiting on a handful of customers.

Olderson moved purposefully toward the enclosure, Gannon a step behind him. At sight of Olderson, Maydet broke off his conversation with the two men and tilted his head toward the gate, a gesture of dismissal. Cleff looked over his shoulder and rose as the two men passed him, but Maydet, feet still atop the desk, did not move. With a kind of kingly indifference, he nodded and said, "Morning, Mr. Olderson."

Olderson pushed past Cleff, and now that he was in company domain and sure of himself, he took the cigar from his mouth and said flatly, "Maydet, I want your books, your inventory of company property, all cash and keys turned over to me by this afternoon."

Maydet said nothing for a moment, only regarded Olderson impassively. Then he said, "Why?"

"You are dismissed as division superintendent, as of today."

Gannon saw the swift anger tighten Cleff's loose

lips, the wild disbelief mount in his eyes, and now Maydet looked at Cleff. Then he returned his glance to Olderson, slowly lifted his feet off the desk, placed them wide apart on the floor, and put a hand on each knee.

"If you mean that, Mr. Olderson, you can get your stage station out of my store by this afternoon. You can get your horses out of my corrals, your feed out of my barns, your crew out of my bunkhouse, and your cook and food out of my kitchen. You can also get yourself out of my town."

"I'll get myself out of your town when you've accounted for all company property and all United States mail," Olderson said grimly. "As for moving that property, I'm prepared to lease what we occupy. If we do lease, all Midland property will be under the direction of the new division superintendent."

Maydet's impassive glance touched Gannon, and then he asked, "That him behind you?"

"That's right. Will Gannon is the name," Olderson said.

Maydet leaned back in his chair, scowling. "Seems like a man should have more notice than this."

Olderson said grimly, "Maydet, did you know a man was murdered in his hotel room last night?"

"I heard," Maydet said, almost with indifference. "That's why they make pistols, so a man can't do that to you."

"You just called this your town," Olderson said coldly. "Is there no law in it?"

"That's not my hotel. That's leased. With a dozen stages and a hundred riders in and out of here every day, how am I to watch the bad ones?" His scowl deepened. "Is that why you're getting rid of me?"

"That decided it," Olderson conceded. "That and the fact that you can't run a stage line, Maydet. You can't move people safely. You can't move mail at all. You can't protect your stock or your employees. You can't even feed them."

"And Gannon can?"

"Yes, he can," Gannon put in quietly.

"And how do you propose to start?" Maydet asked.

"By paying off every man who works for the line in Louisburg," Gannon said quietly. He saw the chill malice in Maydet's eyes and he knew that he had perhaps unnecessarily added to the man's humiliation. Still, he wanted no misunderstanding.

Olderson said then, "We're not discussing my choice of superintendent, Maydet. I know all our space here is leased from you, simply because you were here first and it was easier to lease than build. Still, we're prepared to build if we have to, either east of you or west of you. Would you like to hear my terms?"

Maydet said nothing, as if to imply that he did not care.

"We'll continue to lease all property on the same terms as before, everything to remain the same except your salary, which won't exist. We'll staff this home station ourselves. This is to be a landlord-tenant agreement, nothing more."

Maydet shrugged and he stared musingly at the floor. Will knew what was warring in the man's mind. Midland was paying him a good sum of money yearly for the facilities they used, money which he

did not want to lose. Yet his pride was edging him to
tell Olderson that he could take his stage offices and
corrals elsewhere.

Olderson palmed a heavy gold watch from the
pocket of the knitted vest under his coat and said,
"If you're willing to deal, then let's write up a new
contract that omits your salary but leases your property." He snapped open the watch case, looked at
the time, and said grimly, "I have a funeral to attend
at ten o'clock."

Maydet looked up at him and said thinly, "You
don't leave me much choice, Mr. Olderson."

"You have the widest choice," Olderson contra-
dicted flatly. "You can lease or not lease."

Gannon thought he heard Maydet sigh, and then
the man made a loose gesture with his hand. "Take
a chair then," he said.

As Olderson moved to the chair, Gannon turned
away, his glance touching Cleff. It surprised Cleff
studying him, as if taking the measure of the man
who was now the new division superintendent, not
the emergency stage driver.

Leaving Olderson to his business, Gannon cruised
down the store aisle, noting the filthy cubbyhole office containing only a desk and a safe at the rear of
the storeroom door. This building, he reckoned,
would house his business for some time to come and
he had seen worse. It was out of the weather, conve-
nient to passenger food, lodging, and drink, and was
familiar to every traveler. Heading toward the front,
he noticed the pile of overdue mail sacks stacked
head high behind the counter. Once outside, he
halted in the chill morning and regarded the clutter
of outbuildings lying under the massive bare cotton-

woods to the East. He observed the corrals, barns, blacksmith shop, and wagon sheds, all constructed from cedar wood logs hauled from long distances. Olderson had made a bold brag when he said the line would replace these if necessary, Will guessed, for much labor and expense had gone into their building.

Now Gannon's thoughts turned toward the problems ahead of him. He had declared his intentions of firing all of Maydet's stage line employees and replacing them with his own. At the moment he did not know a single man in Louisburg who could work for him. On impulse then, remembering Hutch, he tramped up to the saloon and went inside, inquiring of the bartender if Hutch Forney was still around.

"He took off after the game broke up last night," the bartender informed him.

No help there, Gannon thought, and he knew that he must send for Hutch by the first westbound stage driver.

Outside, he took out his pipe and reached in his pocket for tobacco. Then, remembering that he had left the tobacco in his room, he headed for the hotel. Angling across the street, he noticed Cleff standing on the puncheon walk before Maydet's store. Cleff watched him cross the street and go up the hotel steps. Once in the lobby, Will moved over to the window and saw Cleff heading for the saloon. He knew the bartender would pass on to Cleff the information that Will had inquired after Hutch and that Cleff would draw his own conclusions. From now on, Will knew, his every action would be watched by Cleff and reported to Maydet. He further knew he must never forget Maydet's boast that this was his town.

Motionless, he considered what he could expect from Cleff. Over the years he had learned to read men who opposed him, mentally tagging them as nothing much to bother with or as real trouble. Cleff was real trouble, Will judged. Without Maydet both to direct and protect him, Cleff would have been dead long ago. There was a wildness in the man's eyes that alerted Will; he sensed the danger in Cleff as he could sense it is a bad horse or a treacherous dog. It was some primal warning of nature. Cleff would be reckless, a fighter, a man of deep hatreds and savage pride. He had seen his boss demoted and humiliated, and even now Will knew Cleff would cheerfully kill him. Only Maydet checked him. Will knew, with a dark certainty, that much of his future lay in Maydet's temper, and that Cleff, the executioner, was the man to watch as a gauge of that temper.

Turning now, he headed toward the stairs and then saw young Dickert sitting in one of the lobby chairs. The boy smiled and nodded at him, and Will halted, saying, "Anything you need?"

Immediately the boy came to his feet. "No, sir, I'm fine, Mr. Gannon."

Will wondered where the lad had picked up his name, and now he studied him. He guessed him to be around sixteen, and someone, somewhere, had taught him manners. Under Gannon's cool appraisal he was not uneasy; he was slight and thin, but there was a set to his jaw which told Will that he was in a hurry to become a man.

Will said, "How are you fixed for money?"

A faint flush touched young Dickert's cheeks, and he said, "Mr. Olderson saw to that, sir. He's taken care of my stage fare."

"To where?" Will's question held only friendly curiosity.

"To the railhead up north and to Indiana."

"Your family's there?"

"Not close family, sir."

Will scowled. "What do you plan back there?"

"I—I don't rightly know, sir. Maybe one of my uncle's friends can find something for me."

"You like the idea of going back?"

The boy considered this question, puzzlement showing in his lean face. "It's about the only place I know," he answered simply.

"Want to work for me, here?" Will asked. "I'll tell you what you'd do and you think about it." He explained then that this was a home station, one of the largest, and would be the division superintendent's headquarters. There would be a division agent who would have charge of all property and stock. He would buy hay and grain, hire the drivers, stocktenders, blacksmiths, and carpenters. In view of the size of the station and the fact that it would be the superintendent's headquarters, the division agent would need help in bookkeeping, ticket sales, inventory, and mail sorting—in fact, he would need help in the housekeeping end while he himself kept his division operating. So would the superintendent. Dickert's pay as helper would be seventy-five dollars a month.

"Is Mr. Olderson the division superintendent?" Dickert asked.

"I am," Gannon said.

A fleeting look of pleasure touched the boy's face, and Will said, "You think about it. I'll see you after the funeral."

"Yes, sir," Dickert said.

"By the way, I don't know your first name."

"It's Bert, Mr. Gannon."

Will nodded pleasantly and turned away. Then he checked himself and went back to young Dickert. "Bert, I was asleep most of the time after we left Lennor's station yesterday. Did the new driver and the big man with him talk much to your uncle?"

Bert nodded. "They asked Uncle Al if he'd like to ride in the box. He took a turn with the driver and so did I." He paused. "Does that mean anything?"

"Probably not," Will said mildly, and headed for the stairs. On the other hand, he was thinking, it could. Travelers talked, and in talking they revealed their degree of prosperity. Maybe Uncle Al yesterday afternoon had talked himself into his grave.

After the funeral Will got his answer from young Dickert. He would stay. Will turned him over to Olderson, who was returning for a session of inventory check with Maydet. Leaving the two at Maydet's store, Will went down to the log blacksmith's shop under the big cottonwoods and there inquired the name of the head stocktender.

He was told the man went only by the name of Rufe and could probably be found in the carpenter shop.

Will found him in the long wagon sheds housing the idle coaches and those in for repair. He was a small man, so dirty that Will could smell the stable stench about him as he approached. Rufe was talking to a carpenter who was working over a long thorough brace gripped in two vises.

"Rufe?" Gannon asked.

The man looked at him insolently and nodded.

"I'm Gannon, the new division superintendent. Make up a messenger coach right away and pull it up before Maydet's store. Throw in five sacks of corn to be put off at the Dry Creek Station. Then start thirty head of horses for the Dry Creek Station and tell the men I'll join them later in the day."

As Gannon talked he saw the disbelief mounting in Rufe's eyes, and when he finished Rufe turned his head aside and spat. "Maydet's my boss and that'll have to be in writing."

It may as well start here, Gannon thought. With his left hand he reached out and caught the man's filthy shirt in his fist, turning him. With his unfisted right hand he clouted Rufe's jaw with a force that sent Rufe staggering back to trip over a stage tongue and sprawl in the dirt.

Slowly Gannon walked over to him as Rufe, shaking his head, scrambled to his feet.

Gannon said softly, "Either I'm your boss or you've got no boss, and I won't put that in writing."

The truculence was gone from Rufe's eyes as he rose, rubbing his jaw. He held his sullen silence as Gannon went on, "When you're finished with that, start a load of hay and grain for Dry Creek."

Rufe asked solemnly, "Do I clear this with Maydet?"

"As far as you're concerned there is no Maydet. Pass that word around to the company help." When Rufe nodded, Will said, "Now show me the saddle horses."

Will turned and tramped out. At one of the many corrals, Rufe halted and Will looked at the dozen horses who were eyeing him curiously. He studied them in silence for several minutes and then said, "Cut out that big chestnut and tie him in front of Maydet's."

"That's Maydet's horse," Rufe said.

Will looked at him. "His or the company's?"

"The company's."

"Tie him in front of Maydet's," Will repeated.

Back at the hotel, Will took the few belongings he would need, rolled them in his blankets, then hoisted his saddle with its rifle and saddle scabbard on his shoulder, picked up his valise, and went downstairs. After arranging for the storage of his valise, he stepped out again into the raw morning. The messenger coach had not yet arrived, but as he made his way across the street among the idling crowd, he saw the chestnut at Maydet's tie-rail. Moving all these people west more quickly was his problem now, and he wished impatiently for Hutch. More coaches would have to be put on, or ordered, and more stock purchased. Men like Rufe would have to be disciplined or replaced, and only Hutch could advise him. But first things must come first, and relieving the Dry Creek Station was the most immediate need, he knew.

Approaching the chestnut, he reached out and gently scratched the pony's neck and nose, talking to him, getting him used to his touch and to his voice before saddling him. Glancing across the horse's neck, he saw Cleff, the point of his shoulder against Maydet's store, watching him. Will finished saddling up and swung under the tie-rail, heading for

Maydet's. As he approached Cleff he saw the malice in the man's eyes. He halted and asked softly, "Any objections?"

"No objections," Cleff answered just as softly.

Will nodded toward the chestnut. "Did I make a mistake?"

Cleff straightened, saying idly, "When you do, you'll know it," and he moved on down the plank walk.

As he entered Maydet's he saw the messenger coach pull away from the wagon sheds. Catching the eye of Olderson, who was talking with Maydet, Will motioned with his head and Olderson excused himself from Maydet to come over.

"When do you get out of here, Mr. Olderson?" Will asked.

Olderson sighed. "Not soon, Will. Maydet's accounts don't exist. I'll have to wait on a copy of our inventory to get here from Salt Lake. He's fighting every item, and without it I'm helpless. Why do you ask?"

Will told him then what he had done already to relieve the emergency at Dry Creek Station and of his wish to talk with Hutch about which men to keep and which to replace. Sending for Hutch would leave Hutch's Helper Creek Station unattended, so he was going to Hutch instead. Could Olderson, with young Dickert's help, hold down the Louisburg end until he could see Hutch and straighten out the affairs in this easternmost point of the three divisions?

Olderson nodded. "I'll stay until you're back, Will. Take the time you need."

Outside the messenger coach was pulled alongside

a break in the tie-rail, the driver boredly lounging against the wheel. He was a bearded man, past middle age, wearing a buttonless and filthy canvas duster, and his cheeks above his beard were sun-browned leather. He had hard-bitten pale eyes that examined Gannon closely as he approached.

Will halted. "I'm Gannon, the new—"

"I know," the driver said. "Name's Wilsey Kirk." He did not offer to shake hands, Will noticed. The news of his set-to with Rufe was already abroad, he guessed.

"Tell the express messenger I want all the backed-up mail sacks cleaned up," Will said. "Pick them up until you're loaded and then go straight through."

Kirk only nodded.

"Another thing," Will went on. "The next driver that uses mail sacks to make a road through boggy places or blow sand has lost his job. Pass that on."

Wilsey Kirk looked at him carefully. "I never used a mail sack to make a road in my life. You pass it on. You're the boss."

Will smiled faintly, liking the man's feisty reply. "Let's both do it," he said mildly, and moved over to his horse.

The messenger coach passed him three miles out on the prairie and in another half-hour Will picked up the thirty horses headed for Dry Creek being loose-herded by two stocktenders. Will took up the swing position to the windward side of the horses, out of the dust, and settled his chestnut into the mile-eating pace of the loose horses.

His thoughts turned now to Hutch and his position with the company. Much as he liked Hutch, he knew he was too reckless and too fiddle-footed for the job of division agent for Division One to replace Maydet. Rather, he would have to rely on Hutch's recommendations. As soon as the affairs of Division One were in order then he would move on to the other two between Rock Creek and Salt Lake, but the affairs here were the more urgent.

The horse herd reached Hutch's Helper Creek swing station in mid-afternoon. While the horses were drinking at the trough by Hutch's corral, Gannon reined aside and pulled up on the hard-packed dirt apron in front of Hutch's sod-roofed log shack. As he dismounted and moved toward the house a woman, unmistakably Indian, stepped into the doorway. She was young and once had been pretty, but now her looks were lost in a sheath of flabby flesh. There was a naked youngster on her hip and she was unmistakably pregnant, Gannon saw. She regarded him in the watchful silence an Indian reserves for a strange white man.

"Hutch in, Mrs. Forney?"

"He's hunting," the woman said.

Gannon scowled. "Who's making up for the east-bound?"

"He got a man to come in," Mrs. Forney said. She gestured with her chin toward the sod barn and its adjoining corrals where a third man was talking to the two stocktenders. A swift irritation came to Gannon then. Hutch had spent last night playing poker, which meant he had not made the change for the eastbound yesterday. Today he was hunting and out of reach. Gannon would have to spend hours waiting for him, perhaps the night. The thought of spending it with this strange and alien woman did not appeal to him and he came to his sudden decision.

"I'm going on to Lennor's, Mrs. Forney. Tell Hutch to come over there when he gets in. Tell him the division superintendent sent for him."

Mounting, he felt a sudden relief. At least Lennor's was clean and the food good.

The eastbound coach passed them in mid-afternoon and Will noted that even the top seats were loaded. It was almost dark, the mountains hulking blackly in the west, when they picked up pin-point lamplight at Lennor's.

Will sent one of his riders ahead to prepare Lennor for their coming and when they finally drove the horse herd onto the station property, Lennor had the corral gate open and a lantern hanging above the watering trough against the barn.

Will was dismounted and was unsaddling his horse when Lennor came up to him.

"Wilsey says you're the new super," Lennor said. His stern face held an expression of satisfaction.

"That's right."

"Maybe things'll be different now," Lennor said soberly.

"They'll either be better or worse, but they won't be the same," Will said. He turned his pony into the corral and together he and Lennor headed for the house, leaving the stocktenders to feed the horses.

Crossing the road, Will thought how warm and welcome this place would seem to a weary traveler, with its clean white paint, lit by the soft lamplight.

Stepping inside ahead of Lennor, Will saw that the room although lamplit was empty.

"Supper's in the kitchen. Easier on the women

folks," Lennor observed. He led the way into the big kitchen where the girl was standing over a big black iron range. She looked up and greeted him unsmilingly, and then Lennor introduced Gannon to his wife, who was setting places at the oilcloth-covered kitchen table. He did not bother to introduce the girl, Will noticed. Lennor's wife was a big-boned, plain woman, clean, unpretty, and as stern-visaged as her husband.

Will was washing up at the basin on the bench beside the back door when the two stocktenders rounded the house. They were, he knew, as dirty and as hungry as he was.

Inside, Lennor had gone about his business, leaving the women to serve the meal. Or rather the girl, Will thought, for Mrs. Lennor had planted herself on a chair in the corner and watched the three men wolf down their meal. Will remembered his last meeting with the girl which, he now conceded, had been unpleasant for them both.

Watching her, he saw the numerous patches in her plain dress and as she silently cleared away the dishes he noted that her small hands were rough and work-hardened.

The stocktenders bolted their meal and then vanished toward the bunkhouse. Will reached in his pocket for his pipe, packed it with a shaggy black tobacco from a deerskin pouch, and only then remembered. He glanced at Mrs. Lennor and said, "Do you mind my pipe?"

"No, Mr. Gannon," she said. Then she rose, looked at the girl, and said, "It's your bedtime, Carrie."

"I'll just tidy up," Carrie said.

Mrs. Lennor left the room and Will lighted his pipe, watching the girl's swift and capable movements, feeling, too, her indifference to him.

"Did this pipe chase her out?" Will asked idly, making conversation.

"No, the men were gone," Carrie answered over her shoulder.

Will frowned. "What does that mean?"

Not looking at him, Carrie answered, "She won't leave me alone with men."

"What am I?" Will asked drily.

"You're the new division superintendent. You're different." Now she looked at him and added slyly, "You've been honored—if it is an honor."

Will ignored this. "What's the matter with men?"

"Everything, according to her. There's no such thing as a good man."

Will thought of Marian then, and he said, "Or a good woman. Which is it that troubles your mother?"

Slowly Carrie turned from the stove and Will saw the anger in her eyes. "Do you mean does she trust me? Probably not. Does she trust you? Probably not. But now we work for you. All of us, you see, must accept your rough remarks now."

Gannon felt his face flushing. "No offense intended," he said.

"But some taken," Carrie said tartly.

She looked away from him now, moved over to the table and began clearing it, ignoring him.

Will pulled on his pipe, watching her, wanting to be pleasant and yet not wanting to seem to apologize. Presently he asked, "Does your father feel about men and you the same way your mother does?''

Carrie said quietly, without looking at him, "He is not my father and she is not my mother. Yes, they both feel that way about men and me."

Will frowned. "How do you come to be here?"

Carrie spoke almost tonelessly. "My family was with an immigrant train that was attacked by Indians east of Louisburg. Both mother and father were killed, and I was just a burden to the rest of them. Besides, after that there was no point going anywhere. When the train stopped here to water the stock, I asked the Lennors for work. They looked like good people and they are."

"But a dull place for a girl," Will observed. Carrie poured some water from the bucket into the dishpan and then looked at him, her green eyes reflective. "Not always. You're meeting different people every day. The whole world goes past you."

"While you stand still," Will said.

Carrie sighed faintly. "Yes, there's that." Her mouth was open to say more, but her glance shuttled to the doorway from the living room.

Lennor entered the kitchen, Will's blanket roll under his arm.

"You won't need these tonight, but I thought you might want some of your gear." Gannon thanked him and Lennor went on, "Your room's upstairs and to the right."

"No. I'll take the bunkhouse," Gannon said.

Lennor shook his head stubbornly. "The wife won't hear of it. She's been fussing with that room ever since Wilsey told us you were on your way."

Gannon rose, knocked out his pipe into his palm,

then moved over to the stove next to Carrie. He lifted the stove lid and dumped the dottle onto the coals. He was at once aware of the woman scent of Carrie's hair and the clean smell of soap, and he turned away, disturbed.

Lennor had gone out and now Will moved to the corner chair and picked up his blanket roll. Halting, he looked at Carrie.

"If the name isn't Lennor, what is it?"

"Carrie Bentall."

"Then good night, Carrie."

Upstairs he found the lamp lighted in his small room. It held a washstand with basin and pitcher, a straight-back chair, and a rope bed whose frame was probably cut from the vast walnut forests of Illinois. Will shucked out of his coat and boots and pulled the chair next to the bed, placing his pipe, matches, and tobacco on it. Then he blew the lamp and lay down. Someone, probably Lennor, was prowling the barn lot with a lantern, for the faintest of light showed on the batten ceiling and then vanished.

The scent he had caught of Carrie's hair in the kitchen still seemed to linger and he wondered why it should disturb him. He knew then that it was because of its strangeness; he had not been even close to a woman in the three months since Marian had left him. Memory of her, unwelcome as it was, came unbidden now and the image of her shaped in his mind. Smaller than the Bentall girl downstairs, as dark as she was fair, but restless with a slashing temper, a creature of moods and passion, and of little patience. When had it gone wrong, he wondered? *Why did she leave?* he asked himself, feeling again the pure misery of the question.

He reached for his pipe and packed it, thinking to change his mood, but the darkness and the solitude only deepened it. He supposed she had met this man on one of her many trips to San Francisco where, to soothe her restlessness, he allowed her to go. The last time she had overstayed her promised date of return, but the following day the letter told him why. She was leaving him to live with a man she would not name, and she did not care a damn for the conventions, she wrote. She wanted nothing from home to remind her that she had once been his wife. There was no sense, she wrote, in his trying to seek her out. If he brought her back, she would kill herself. The letter was written in hysteria, Will judged, but there was no mistaking her feelings. Quiet investigation by one of his friends in the San Francisco office of the company revealed that Marian was living with a man who owned several coastal schooners, and Will made no effort to see her or to persuade her to return. She had found a man who would give her something he could not, and with characteristic selfishness she had deserted him for this man. Without any doubt she was fickle, selfish, wrongheaded, and wronghearted, but he loved her as he would never love another woman.

When the very rooms in which he lived, the very furniture he touched, the plates from which he ate became intolerable to him because they reminded him of her, he had left, knowing that never again would any woman be in a position to hurt him as Marian had.

He fumbled for the chair beside his bed, found it, and laid his pipe upon it and stared at the ceiling, his body wanting sleep, his mind refusing it. Then he

realized that he could dimly see the outline of the
battens above him and he scowled in the darkness,
wondering at the source of light. He wondered, too,
at the racket the horses were kicking up. Rising, he
looked out the window. Across the road, flames
were licking under the eaves of the hay barn.

By the light of the fire, Will could dimly make out
the figure of a man on the far side of the corral,
waving a coat in an effort to stampede the milling,
terrified horses in the corral next the barn.

Moving swiftly, Will reached out for his gun hanging in its holster on the back of the chair. Rounding
the bed, he touched the window and raised it. Then
he aimed at the moving figure and fired. On the heel
of his shot came the flatter, louder report of a rifle
fired from downstairs.

Will was already in motion. Ignoring his boots, he
climbed out on the porch roof, rammed the gun in
his waistband, swung over the edge of the roof, and
dropped the four feet to the ground. He was running
as he landed and he heard someone yank open the
door behind him.

The horses, now that the barn was afire, were in a
panic of fear. He could hear them pawing and kicking at the corral as they milled and fought each
other.

Running desperately now, ignoring the bite of the
stones under his sock feet, Will dodged around a
wagon, rounded the corner of the corral, and
achieved the corral gate. A horse had reared until
his forefeet were over the top bar but he was pinned
by the horse flesh piling behind him. Will drew back
the bar, then heaved the gate open, at the same time

wheeling flat against the corral out of the way of the
terror-stricken horses stampeding past him.

He felt the solid gate posts shudder as the horses,
squealing and savagely grunting, fought each other
to be free of the fire behind them.

Turning his head, Will saw that Lennor too, rifle
in hand, had flattened against the corral a few feet
away. Then the corral was empty and Will turned to
look at the blazing barn. Lennor, however, did not
pause to watch; he circled past the open gate and
Will, knowing where Lennor was going, fell in behind him. Rounding the far corner of the corral,
Lennor hauled up so abruptly that Will bumped into
him. There, face-down in the dirt, his hands still
clutching his coat, lay a man.

Lennor and Will approached together, but it was
Will who knelt and turned the man over. The shot
had caught him in the chest and he must have died
instantly. The dirt was pooled with his blood.

Will looked up at Lennor, but he had turned away
to retch against the corral fence. Rising, Will waited,
and when Lennor turned, Will saw with surprise a
look of sick anguish in the man's face.

"May God forgive me," Lennor said quietly. "I
have taken a man's life."

Watching him, Will knew that Lennor's remorse
was real and he said quietly, "He was dead before
you shot, Lennor."

The older man looked at him searchingly.

"I shot from my bedroom. I saw my shot turn him
and he was falling as you shot." This was not true,
for Will knew he had missed the man. But besides
wishing to spare Lennor, Will saw how this would
work for him.

A shuddering relief seemed to come to Lennor, and now the stocktenders arrived out of breath.

"Let's get what we can out of the barn," Will directed.

Working feverishly under the loft whose timbers were glowing a cherry red, the five men moved most of Lennor's gear out into the barn lot. They were returning for the big forge bellows when Will called, "Look out!" The two stocktenders dashed out just as the loft timbers gave way in a great gout of fire and sparks.

Lennor had so spaced his other buildings that none of them were threatened by the fire. Nevertheless Will posted a stocktender on the roof of the low wagon shed and the old stables. The fiercely blazing barn lit up the surrounding night and Will could see Mrs. Lennor and Carrie watching from the porch.

He tramped back to the dead man and halted, looking down at him, wondering. Lennor came up beside him, and this time, knowing that he had not brought about the man's death, Lennor looked at him.

"Know him?" Will asked.

Lennor shook his head. One of the stocktenders Will had brought with him, a lanky, taciturn boy of sixteen, came up now and Will asked his question.

"Who is he?"

"Name's Ahearn," the boy said.

"Does he work for Maydet?"

The boy nodded. "Odd jobs and such."

This then was Maydet's first move and it could have been a crippling one if the horses had been lost. As it was, the loose horses would graze close by and could easily be rounded up in the morning, and

Lennor's barn could be replaced at nominal cost. Maydet had failed to hurt them seriously and his own man had been killed. Will considered this with grim pleasure. Maydet would learn that any move against the line brought savage retaliation, which was what Will wanted.

Carrie was up at first light and from her tiny room off the kitchen she saw the stocktenders leave the bunkhouse for the stables on their way to round up the stampeded horses. On her way to the stack of kindling and wood stacked outside the back door, Carrie paused to gauge the coming morning. There was the fresh smell of the grass, but mingled with it was the bitter, all-pervasive smell of burnt wood.

Rounding the corner of the house, she looked across the road at the still smoking ashes of the stables. She shivered slightly and did not know if it was from the chill of the morning or from the memory of last night's violence. Lying in the old stables was a man who would be buried today, with the heart torn out of him by a bullet. This was her first nearness to death since the nightmare ambush that took the lives of her parents, and she found that she still could not accept any death with indifference.

Gathering an armload of wood, she stepped back into the kitchen, built the fire, and set about making the batter from the sour-dough starter at the back of the old range. She worked expertly, her chores memorized and done by rote so that they did not interfere with her thoughts. The night's happenings were still close to her and in the solitude of the kitchen she considered them.

There was Gannon, the new superintendent who

had killed a man and afterwards slept calmly. He was surly enough, Carrie judged, and a man who seemed to like his own grey thoughts. Somehow the unexpected sharp turns of his speech made her uneasy and she wondered what it was in his manner that made her feel he held her in quiet contempt. Now she could hear the Lennors stirring above stairs and she knew that this half-hour of pleasant solitude would soon end.

Mrs. Lennor came into the kitchen, gave Carrie a cheerless good morning, and set about helping her. She was followed by Mr. Lennor who, once his chore of grinding the roasted coffee beans was finished, sat down to await his breakfast. Both of them, Carrie thought without bitterness, seemed to regard her as they regarded their furniture; she was something to walk around and to be treated with that respect due anything of value. She could not help but compare them with her noisy, impractical, generous father and her bright and lively mother.

When his food was placed before him, Lennor said grace, and Carrie, standing at the stove, bowed her head as she had been instructed to do. During breakfast the Lennors talked of the loss of the barn and speculated on whether or not the company would help them replace it. Carrie took no part in the conversation, but instead planned for the mid-morning meal she would be serving the eastbound stage passengers.

Once breakfast was finished, Carrie cleared the table and started to prepare for the second wave of breakfasts. Presently Gannon came into the kitchen, said, "Morning, Carrie," and sat down. His black hair had been wet and, as she served him Carrie noted streaks of grey in it. Turning back to the stove, she heard the front door open and footsteps approaching. Glancing up, she saw Hutch Forney, a pleasant grin on his handsome face, come to a halt in the doorway. He was about to speak when his glance settled on Gannon and she saw the surprise wash over his face.

"Will!" Hutch said slowly, in quiet amazement. "I thought you were headed east." Hutch came into the room, saying belatedly, "Morning, Carrie," and then halted beside Gannon.

"I sent for you," Will said.

"You sent for me?" Hutch echoed, wonderingly. "Maydet sent word to come over."

Gannon said drily, "If you'd tend your station, Hutch, you'd know what's happening. I left word with your wife that the division super wanted to see you."

It took only a second for Hutch to understand, and then he flushed. "You're the new division super, then."

Gannon nodded as Carrie moved over to set a place for Hutch.

"Your food's ready as soon as you wash up, Hutch," she said.

Hutch threw his hat on the chair as he stepped out the back door and now Carrie looked at Gannon with a new curiosity. Where and how had he known Hutch Forney, the improvident squaw man who ran a swing station east?

When Hutch returned and sat down to the table, Gannon had finished his breakfast and was packing his pipe. As Carrie served Hutch, he looked up at her. "Did Lennor lose much in the fire, Carrie?"

Glancing at Gannon, Carrie said, "No, but another man did."

Hutch looked puzzled and shuttled his glance to Gannon, who was looking at Carrie.

Then Gannon said, "She means that one of Maydet's crew was killed last night, a man name of Ahearn."

As Carrie turned away, Gannon briefly told Hutch of last night's happening. Carrie noted that he spoke almost casually of downing Ahearn with a shot from the upstairs window. It was all true and accurate, but his words were callous in a way that she could not define.

"So Maydet's paying you off already," Hutch said.

"We'll talk about that later," Gannon said flatly. "Let's talk about you now."

"What about me?" Hutch demanded.

"The line pays you swing station people for two reasons—you're handy and you're reliable. When you get unreliable, we change."

"You're talking about me?" Hutch asked.

"I am. If we wanted a half-breed to feed and shape up our stock and mend our harnesses, we'd hire him, not you."

Carrie looked at Hutch. She saw that his neck was red, but he was only looking at the plate.

"I know for certain that in the last three days you've only stopped at your place to pick up or leave a gun, Hutch." Gannon's voice was cold, flat. "What'll it be?"

Hutch said softly, "You stopped by my place, Will. What did you see?"

Carrie saw Gannon frown. "Your wife and child."

"That's what I mean," Hutch said. "Both black-eyed and coffee-colored and smelling like a bonfire. Would you like to stay home with that?"

"Whose fault is that?" Gannon countered.

"Mine, but I don't have to like it."

"And I don't like it the other way," Gannon said. "Dog it any more, Hutch, and you're through. What'll it be?"

Carrie felt her body tense. Gannon's rough words were calculated to anger Hutch, and she knew that Hutch Forney had a reputation for both temper and violent action.

The two men regarded each other a long moment and then Gannon said softly, "I want an answer now, Hutch."

Hutch said thinly, "I'm still working for you."

Gannon nodded satisfied, then said idly, "Maybe as a horse buyer. That'll keep you away from home." Gannon rose and said, "Finish up. You'll ride with me today," and he tramped out of the room.

Carrie found she'd been holding her breath. When Gannon had left the room, she looked at Hutch, a kind of angry bewilderment in her. In a matter of seconds Gannon had turned from a hard, relentless man who must win his point, into a man who, having won it, could be easy and generous.

Hutch glanced up from his plate and surprised her watching him. The little dancing lights of anger had not entirely faded from Hutch's green eyes.

"He can push a man," Hutch said softly.

"Some men," Carrie corrected him angrily.

"No, any man."

3

Leaving the stocktenders to help Lennor bury Ahearn and begin the raising of a new barn, Will and Hutch moved on west with the horse herd. That day they passed two plodding immigrant trains before they met the eastbound stage whose driver, his teams exhausted through lack of replacements at the Dry Creek Station, had set his passengers to walking. Fresh teams were cut out of the herd and hooked to the stage and the herd continued west, held to a slower pace now by the weary horses that had been exchanged. It was after dark when they drove the herd into the corral at Dry Creek Station, after first being challenged from the dark adobe by Keefe, rifle in hand.

Keefe preceded them into the dark shack and lit a candle, then turned to look at his visitors. He looked at Gannon a long moment and then said, "I've seen you, but where?"

"The morning your stock was run off. I was driving the eastbound."

"He's your new boss," Hutch said drily.

Keefe's face, gaunt and covered with beard stubble, tightened at the jaw hinge. "You're Gannon, then. All right, Mr. Gannon, give me a paper to the division agent. I'm heading for Louisburg tomorrow to pick up my wages and clear out."

"All right," Gannon said mildly. He looked about the mean room which held only the barest essentials —a straw pallet, a cracked stove, a puncheon table, and a candle box nailed to the wall for a cupboard. Rounds of logs made up the three chairs, and all the clothes Keefe possessed hung from a single nail over the pallet.

"You'll get some good eating, too, Mr. Super," Keefe said, anger smouldering in his eyes. "The company supplies beans and bannock and creek water."

Will nodded.

"But you'll be warm because I've got plenty of wood chopped," Keefe went on, still watching Gannon. "I've had no stock to feed, no teams to change, and nothing but time on my hands."

"Things'll be different," Gannon said quietly.

"They'll sure as hell be different for me," Keefe said flatly. "No more sleeping with a rifle. No more fighting with drivers. No more messengers cussing me. No more watching horses starve. No more of me starving either." He turned to the stack of wood and stoked the stove, moving a black pot forward to heat up. Will saw that his hands were trembling with anger and felt a sudden pity for this boy. The victim of Maydet's neglect and indifference, he still had been loyal enough to stay until he could be replaced.

What Keefe said was literally true. Their supper consisted of beans, bannock, and water, a satisfying meal but one which Gannon knew could become monotonous. Finished, they cleaned up the few dishes and then Gannon began quizzing Hutch on a reliable man for division agent. Keefe listened moodily to the talk as Will told Hutch his plans. He mentioned, almost casually, that feed and grub was already on its way to the division swing stations, as well as horse replacements where needed.

"What about pay?" Keefe interrupted. "That on the way, too?"

"What's owed you?" Gannon asked.

"Better'n six months."

"That'll come, too, as soon as I get a look at the books." Gannon paused, then asked curiously, "How do you come to be here, Keefe?"

"Riordan and his deaf brother was running the station then and I hired on to cut wild hay. I worked alone until a bunch of Indian scouts spotted me and I had to get out. When Riordan asked Maydet for feed and never got it, him and his brother pulled out." He added bitterly, "I wished I'd gone with 'em."

Hutch asked, "Why didn't you?"

"You can't let stock starve. If I'd turned them loose, the Indians would've got 'em. Besides, you can't run a stage line without stock."

"Did Maydet finally send you feed?" Gannon asked.

"He sent a man out to replace me, name of Ahearn. I chased him off with a gun. I wasn't quitting till I was paid. After that I got my pay and some feed."

Hutch said drily, "Your troubles with Ahearn are over. He's dead."

"When?" Keefe asked.

Hutch told him of Ahearn's attempt to destroy the horse herd last night and of his being killed, and Gannon watched Keefe's face come alert with interest. When Hutch was finished, Keefe shuttled his glance to Gannon.

"This Ahearn's got some tough friends," Keefe said soberly. "They used to stay here when they was hunting, only mostly they drank." He paused. "You better watch out."

"They better watch out," Gannon said flatly. "From now on, the company protects its men and its property. If anybody bothers us, they'll get what Ahearn got."

"But you've got Ahearn's friends working for you."

"Not any more," Gannon said. "This is a stage line now, not one of Maydet's sidelines. We're going to stock it, carry every sack of mail, run on schedule, and keep clean stations. I'll do it if I have to fire every man in three divisions, build new stations, and pay off every driver." Then he added quietly, "I told you it will be different, and it will."

Keefe said nothing, and now Hutch rose and stretched. "I forget what sleep is, but I think I'll lie down and try to remember."

Keefe offered his pallet, but both men refused. They spread their blanket rolls on the dirt floor, and Keefe made sure his rifle was on the floor beside him before he pulled off his boots, blew the candle, and turned into his blankets.

In the darkness Gannon wondered if his patience with the boy would pay off. His interest had seemed to quicken as he had listened to Gannon's plans for the division and maybe, just maybe, he would change his mind, Gannon thought. He wanted men like Keefe, and he knew that with enough of them he could straighten out the division.

Sometime in the night the westbound coach pulled in. Keefe was ready for it, the fresh teams harnessed by lantern light, and the passengers barely had time to stretch their legs before the coach was on its way.

Next morning, after a breakfast of beans and bannock, Gannon packed and lighted his pipe then moved outside and went over to the corral. He leaned against it and regarded the horses, noting their condition. Keefe and Hutch came up and Gannon looked at Keefe. He nodded his head toward the corral and said to Keefe, "Take any one you want except Hutch's grey and my big chestnut. Turn him in at Louisburg."

Keefe nodded, but he was frowning. "You aim to leave them all here?"

Gannon shook his head. "What's the name of the first swing station west?"

"Soderstrom's."

"I'll leave fourteen here and split the rest between Soderstrom and Boley." He straightened up. "Show Hutch the teams you changed last night."

Keefe looked at him, puzzled.

"He'll be holding down the station until I can get a replacement for you."

"But you'll need him to help drive your loose horses, won't you?"

"He'd be a help," Gannon conceded.

"Then take him," Keefe said. "I've waited this long, I reckon I can wait two days longer."

Gannon looked at him and shook his head. "You better get along, Keefe. I won't have a man working for me who doesn't want to, not even for two days. Mr. Olderson will pay you off in Louisburg. You won't need a note from me. Just tell him you're quitting."

Here and now was the choice that was crowding Keefe, and Gannon had purposely stated it flatly. Keefe looked at the horses, scowling, and was silent a moment, deep in thought. Then he looked at Gannon. "You and him go on," he said quietly. "I reckon I'll like working for you."

Gannon felt a pleasant moment of triumph. He had won his small gamble.

That morning they pushed on into the foothills, dropping off eight of the remaining herd at Soderstrom's log ranch house. The teams for the overdue eastbound were already harnessed in the corral, and Mrs. Soderstrom, a strapping Swedish woman who spoke no English, was waiting in the barn lot. Gannon wanted to quiz her on the absence of her husband, but there was no way of communicating with this smiling blond behemoth.

Only minutes after they left Soderstrom's, they met the eastbound Concord on a curve of the winding road. The surprised herd of horses scattered like chaff to either side of the coach, while the driver did not even attempt to brake. Gannon pulled his horse violently to the left, while Hutch roweled his horse up the bank to the right. As the coach bowled through, Hutch cursed wildly at the driver. When the coach was past, Hutch regained the road and looked at Gannon, who was laughing.

"What's funny?" Hutch demanded.

"He's late and he's making up time," Gannon said. "That suits me."

Rounding up their scattered horses, they changed mounts and were soon into the green timber of the mountains. Signs of the spring blizzard had almost vanished; the road was wet and the forest chill with the run-off of the melting snow.

By mid-afternoon they reached Bates Boley's home station and Gannon had his first look at it in daylight. The barn lot was knee-deep in mud and in the corral the horses were bunched against the log stable, in the only dry spot. Bates Boley trotted out from his log house through the litter of his yard. He almost tripped over a rotting deer hide by the door, and when he reached the corral he had an exasperating struggle with the sagging gate before he could open it to let the horses in.

Gannon looked about him with distaste, noting Boley's daughter who had appeared at the door. Boley seemed to have dropped every tool where he had last used it. Cut poles, instead of being stacked for future use, were scattered like jackstraws all around the place. His woodpile was a low mound strewn over half the area between the shack and the edge of the clearing. As their horses picked their way through the litter, a mongrel dog, worrying at a deer head, growled at them.

"Who's she?" Hutch asked, nodding toward the house.

"When I went through here, I figured she was his daughter," Gannon said.

Bates Boley, at the gate, had not shaved since Gannon had seen him last, and Gannon noticed that he had not bothered to wash hands or arms since butchering out the deer whose hide he had almost tripped over.

"You must be Gannon," Boley said. "Been expecting you."

Gannon looked down at him. "Your place doesn't look like it."

Boley looked around him, puzzled.

"You get many people that stop over here, Boley?"

Bates looked at him. "Hardly none."

Gannon gestured toward the littered yard. "No wonder," he said bluntly. "You're living in a pig pen."

He dismounted into the mud and looked into the corral, pooled with water. "Why don't you ditch that so it will drain?"

"Never seem to get the time," Boley said, his voice apologetic.

"Find time," Gannon said coldly. "That's company stock and it's company harness they've been tramping in the mud." He nodded toward a set of harness which had slipped from a corral pole into the mud.

Boley nodded sullenly and Gannon turned and unsaddled. Hutch, he noticed, had already unsaddled, turned his horse in, and was walking toward the house.

"Come on up. Maggie's got food waiting for you," Boley said to Gannon.

Silently Gannon swung in beside him and they tramped across the littered yard. They stepped into the big room holding the two trestle tables. As his glance traveled the room, Gannon noted dirty plates still on the uncleared table and unwashed whiskey cups on the plank bar in the corner. Hutch was standing in the doorway from the kitchen lean-to and Gannon could hear the clatter of tin dishes coming from the kitchen.

* * *

Hutch was regarding Maggie Boley, standing at the stove. She was wearing a drab grey dress and not much under it, Hutch thought. She was a full-bodied girl, perhaps nineteen, and with her head in profile, Hutch could see the pouting dissatisfied lips, the straight nose, and the long eyelashes. Her dark auburn hair was not lately combed, but to Hutch this lent her a kind of raffish informality.

She was suddenly aware that she was being watched and looked up at him. Her eyes, Hutch noted, were a real green, guarded and at the same time bold. She was pretty, Hutch decided, but a sullen, resentful wench and probably lazy too.

Hutch smiled. "Reckon a man could get a drink of water?"

The girl nodded her head toward the bucket on the littered table and then coolly watched him for a moment as he went into the kitchen. He moved with an easy, careless grace to the water bucket.

He took a dipperful of water, and as he slowly sipped it he watched her. She made a self-conscious gesture of brushing her hair from her forehead with her forearm and then swiftly she looked at him. Their glances met and held for a moment, and then the girl said, "What are you staring at?"

Hutch lowered the dipper and grinned. "A pretty girl. I don't know her name though."

Maggie Boley turned her attention to the meat sizzling in the skillet and Hutch saw a faint color come into her cheeks.

"You get on about your business," the girl said.

"It can wait," Hutch murmured. He took another sip of water, watching the girl, mentally daring her to look up. He saw the corner of her mouth lift in a beginning smile.

"Clara Boley?" Hutch asked, his voice musing. "No, that doesn't go with a redhead. Bertha Boley? No, that goes with a cow. Biddy Boley? No, that goes with a hen."

Suddenly the girl giggled and glanced at him, and Hutch could see that a kind of sleepy interest had replaced the sullenness in her eyes. He could hear Gannon's low positive voice in the other room and he knew that Will would be wondering what was keeping him. He set the tin dipper back in the pail and said softly, "Pretty Kitty Boley. It's got to be that."

She did not look at him; he waited for her smile, and when it came he turned and walked back into the main room.

Gannon and Boley had gone into the bunk room and Hutch started back into the kitchen, then hauled up. *Better not,* he thought. He felt a kind of secret excitement riding him. The girl had looks, but beyond that there was something about her that spoke to him in a language he understood, and he knew what it was. Her real nature, Hutch guessed shrewdly, was like his own, restless and reckless. The sullenness didn't deceive him; his soft talk had wiped that out of her eyes and for a moment she had revealed that wildness that he intuitively understood.

Maggie came out of the kitchen carrying two plates and at the same time Gannon and Boley came out of the bunk room. As she crossed the room and set the plates on the table, Hutch noticed that she had combed her hair and he felt his pulse quicken. He had reached her.

Gannon sat down on the bench and Hutch slid in beside him. The meat was hot and tough, the beans cold, and the bread heavy, but they ate hungrily. Boley puttered about the bar, watching them uneasily. They were finishing as Maggie Boley came in with a granite coffee pot and filled their cups. As she turned away, Gannon said, "Just a minute."

Maggie Boley paused and Gannon said, "Come here, Bates."

Boley shuffled over to them, his manner already cringing as he halted by his daughter.

Gannon said flatly, "I haven't eaten since morning, so I'm hungry, but if I got off a stage and you served me that meal I'd throw it in your face."

The girl's face went sullen, Hutch noticed, but Gannon went on mercilessly. "You know how to cook and bake?" he demanded.

The girl nodded, her eyes hating him.

"You know how to sweep and wash?"

Again she nodded.

"You better start doing it," Gannon said, "because I'm going to question passengers at Louisburg. If I get any complaints about the food or about the dirt here, you both can move on." Gannon stood up, and Hutch, watching his face stern in cold anger, thought, *Something's happened to him.* His glance shuttled to the girl; she was staring at the table, angry but submissive.

"Now, Bates, come outside," Gannon said roughly. "I'm going to tell you what you'll change around here." He turned and went toward the door and Boley followed meekly. The girl picked up the dishes and retreated into the kitchen. Hutch rose and followed her, and when he entered the kitchen she looked up at him, her eyes blazing.

"Maybe he'd like to try cooking at all hours of the day and night. Maybe he'd like to clean up after drunken, dirty men."

"Sure, sure," Hutch said soothingly. "That was a good meal."

"You liked it?" Maggie asked, her anger fading.

Hutch nodded. "I know how it is with you. It's hard to cook anything fancy when you're so far away from the stuff to do it with."

Maggie nodded and Hutch moved closer to her.

"Still, I can cook," Maggie said.

Hutch grinned. "You're too pretty to cook good. That should be left to fat women and bald-headed men."

Maggie smiled with pleasure.

"That leaves the rest of us to have fun with each other," Hutch said, grinning.

"Then I bet you're a terrible cook," Maggie said. "What's your name?"

"Hutch, pretty Kitty. What's yours?"

"Margaret."

"Margaret," Hutch echoed. "Meg." He looked her over from head to toe and nodded, grinning. "Yes, that figures—leggy Meg."

Again Maggie giggled. "You're fresh as paint, Mr. Hutch."

"No, I'm just hungry," Hutch murmured.

"But you just ate."

"Not for food, for this." Hutch folded her in his arms and she turned her head to avoid his kiss. Almost roughly he put his hand up under her jaw, turned her head, and kissed her. She struggled at first and then slowly her body relaxed against his and she returned his kiss.

Hutch heard the door in the other room open and he released her, stepping back.

"You liked that. You'll dream about it," he said in a low voice. "So will I. I liked it so much I'll be back."

He winked at her, but before she could speak he turned and went out of the kitchen. He forced himself to make his face bland and uncommunicative and he was whistling a thin tune which would seem to stem from boredom.

Gannon was standing by the open door and he said, "Ready?"

Puzzled, Hutch said, "For what?"

"We're heading back," Gannon said. His dark glance touched Boley at the bar. "I'm like the coach passengers, Bates; I'd rather travel than put up with this."

Gannon turned toward Hutch, saying, "Saddle up, Hutch. I'll pick up some grub."

"I can do it," Hutch said, half turning.

"No," Gannon said flatly. "I want a few more words with Maggie."

Shrugging, Hutch nodded and stepped out. He felt an angry impatience with Gannon as he tramped down toward the corral. If they'd stayed the night he could have seen Maggie again and come to some understanding about the future, unspoken or not. He wanted to learn how carefully Bates Boley watched his daughter and what arrangements they could make to meet, for Hutch was sure this girl would be his.

Minutes later Will left the house carrying a sack of grub and they saddled up and headed back down the road in the beginning dusk. Gannon was silent, preoccupied with his own thoughts. Hutch was content to have it that way. Already he was wondering how he could work it to see Maggie and still run the Helper Creek Station. Yesterday morning Will had said something about letting him buy horses. That would keep him traveling, Hutch knew, but not in this direction. Only when the division stations needed stocking could he come this way, touching Boley's station along with the others of the division. By dark, however, Hutch thought he had it worked out.

An hour later they pulled off the road into the timber alongside a small creek and under a stand of tall spruces they found a dry camp. While Gannon picketed their horses close by and unsaddled, Hutch built a fire and collected wood, marshaling in his mind the facts of his argument.

The deer steaks Maggie had given Gannon were spitted and warmed over the fire, and they, together with the rock-hard slab of bannock, made the meal.

Hutch waited until Gannon's pipe was going and they were sprawled on their blanket rolls beside the fire. Off in the close night they could hear their horses, well fed at Boley's, foraging in the vanishing snow around the perimeter of the circle their picket ropes allowed them to move.

Hutch thumbed his hat off his forehead and asked idly, "How come we didn't keep west, so long as we're this far?"

"One division at a time, Hutch. Once I clean up this one, I'll move on to division two."

Hutch nodded and waited, not wanting to crowd this. Then he said, almost idly, "I got to thinking today about our talk last night at Dry Creek. Remember I told you Hugh Wells might make you a good division agent?"

Gannon nodded.

"I got to thinking I'm a better man than Hugh Wells."

Gannon looked closely at him, his deep-set eyes waiting.

Frowning, Hutch pegged a chunk of bark into the fire and watched it burn, giving Gannon time to turn this over in his mind. Then he went on, "I'm no damn good at Helper Creek, Will. Every time I look at the woman I want to be on the move. I'm willing to keep her and the kid because where else would they go? They're mine and I put 'em here and I reckon I'll take care of 'em." He looked up at Will. "But it's no good, Will."

"I'll need a horse buyer."

"Give me a chance at division agent," Hutch said quietly, earnestly. "I've changed since we were together down south. So have you. You know that."

"Yes," Will said tonelessly.

"All right, I used to raise hell about four feet and tilt it every time I got the chance. The last thing I wanted was responsibility. Now it's different."

"You had responsibility at Helper Creek and dogged it," Gannon pointed out.

"It's not the same," Hutch said vehemently. "If I get away from the woman and the kid I'll stick to my job like paint to a board. I know what I'm doing, Will, and I know what you want me to do. I know stock and I can see it's taken care of. I know as much about a Concord as Abbott and Downing or any carpenter I hire. I know the good drivers and the ones we should let go, and I know the important thing about hay and grain is not buying it but having it where it's needed. I can run this division, Will, and I never saw the day when I'd back water from Maydet."

Everything he said was true, and Will knew it, Hutch thought. He watched Gannon and saw that Will was still withholding judgment, and he asked drily, "Remembering, Will?"

Gannon nodded.

"The time I rolled boulders down into our road camp so that fat-headed captain of our cavalry escort shot up the night for two hours?"

Gannon smiled faintly and nodded. "That and others."

"That's all gone," Hutch said earnestly. "You make me division agent and you won't see any drivers coming up to me in Maydet's saloon to beg for more feed at the swing stations. No station will be short. I'll ride that division until I can run it in my sleep."

Hutch knew he had said enough. Gannon was silent a long while, staring into the fire. Presently he said, almost musingly, "A man usually fires his friends last, but I don't, Hutch. I fire them first because I expect them to deliver more."

"Who's complaining?" Hutch asked quietly.

Gannon took a deep breath. "We'll try it awhile, Hutch. When I ride you, take it, because I'm riding myself."

Hutch grinned swiftly and did not even want to keep his pleasure of this news from showing on his face. He could do Will a good job, he knew, and that would never worry him, but most of his pleasure lay in the fact that he had already announced his intentions of traveling the line, and Will had accepted them. That meant he would have freedom to come and go at Boley's, and since it was a station Gannon himself was concerned about, he could give it—and Maggie Boley—time and attention.

The westbound woke Gannon before daylight. He could hear the harness jingle and the hoof beats of the team digging in on the upgrade. Looking at the stars, he saw that dawn was not far off and he rolled out of his blankets, kicked up the fire, and by daylight they were on their way.

That sunny, still morning, as they rode out of the timber and into the warmer foothills, Will considered his decision of last evening. There had never been any doubt in his mind that Hutch had more than enough knowledge required of a division agent. Nor did he doubt that any driver, stocktender, carpenter, harness maker, or blacksmith could shirk his duty without Hutch knowing it. The trouble was, he knew, that Hutch could sincerely mean what he said while he was saying it, but not mean it at all when delivering became irksome. Still, you couldn't judge a man now by what he was five years ago, or even two. *Not even me,* he thought bleakly, remembering his life with Marian. Maybe what Hutch said was true: that, once free of the company of his Papago wife and half-breed child, he would welcome responsibility.

At midday, they spooked a small herd of antelope to the south, and Hutch, remembering Keefe's shortage of provisions, was all for giving chase. Calculating that the grub he had ordered out of Louisburg would be at Keefe's now, and also remembering that their mounts were not fresh, Gannon decided against pursuit.

An hour later the log shack of the Dry Creek Station, abutting almost the last of the foothills, was in sight. Gannon decided they would change horses here and push on to Lennor's that night, and he discovered that he was looking forward to this with something like pleasure. After the slim fare of the last two days and the cold night, Lennor's with its good food and beds, seemed a haven. He had a mental picture of Carrie Bentall, straight-backed at the stove, the kitchen and common room shining with her cleanliness.

Hutch's voice roused him. "You see any horses?"

Gannon looked ahead at the station corrals, saw them empty and frowned. That meant that the feed on its way from Louisburg had not yet arrived and that Keefe was probably grazing the horses somewhere east on the prairie.

Minutes later they reined up in the hard-packed dirt around the shack. Gannon, before dismounting, sat motionless in his saddle, an uneasiness growing within him. Alongside the bottom pole of one section of the corral he saw wisps of new hay which had been dropped as the feed was forked over. That meant Keefe's feed was already here. His glance shuttled to the shack with its door standing open, and then he saw the stain in the hard-packed grey of the yard. The stain led up to the door and over the sill.

Swiftly Will swung out of the saddle and ran for

the door. He halted in the doorway and peered into the gloomy interior. He saw a shape on the floor beside the pallet and moved into the dark room toward it.

It was Keefe lying face-down on the floor, his rifle still in hand, a circle of darkness under him.

As he knelt, Will heard Hutch's bitter cursing beside him. He turned Keefe over on his back and now brown blood that stained his ragged shirt on his left side was replaced by new blood as the wound opened. Swiftly Hutch and Will lifted him to the straw pallet and pulled off his shirt. The wound seeped slowly and Will knew that Keefe, already close to death, would surely die unless the bleeding was stopped.

Moving over to the cabinet on the wall, Gannon found an opened sack of flour and returned to Keefe. Then he poured the flour onto the wound, stanching the flow of blood. Afterward he looked at Keefe and saw that the boy's face was drained of all color, his lips faintly blue.

Then the anger came to Will, a quiet, murdering wrath. He looked up and found Hutch watching him, and for a helpless moment he knew that Hutch was wordlessly asking what was to be done. Briefly, Will considered what they had to do. The eastbound stage was due soon, and if Keefe was to live he must be moved where he could get some sort of care and attention. That was the first thing to consider, and as Will speculated gravely on moving him, Hutch said quietly, "You think we can get him to my woman, Will?"

Will shook his head. "We'll be lucky if we can get him to Lennor's on the eastbound." He looked at

Keefe again, wondering how long he had lain there slowly bleeding to death, and he thought, *maybe, just maybe.* The raid must have taken place after the westbound stage passed or else Soderstrom would have heard the news from the driver. Even as he was thinking this, Will calculated that the herd was probably stolen around midnight and had a fifteen-hour start. In those fifteen hours Keefe had somehow managed to drag himself off the hard-packed clay into the shack but he had not quite made the straw pallet.

Will pushed his anger aside, considering this latest move of Maydet's, considering what must be done. Finally he said, "Hutch, you take him on the eastbound and turn him over to Lennor's women. Then borrow enough horses from Lennor for a team change and bring them back here. You'll keep the station until I get back."

"You going to try it alone, Will?"

Gannon nodded.

"That's what they want," Hutch said flatly. "This time they don't give a damn about the horses. They want you."

Will scowled. "How do you figure that?"

"They knew you were at this end of the line. They could've picked that up from any driver. If they wanted the horses they'd have waited until you were in Louisburg so they'd have had a three-day head start on you."

It was true, Will knew, but he felt the old stubbornness pushing him. Wisdom dictated that he ignore this thrust of Maydet's and bide his time until the odds were closer to even. He would be alone, his horse was already tired, and he had no chance of replacing him. Beyond that, he did not know how many men he was up against. But if he ignored this, then no station and no employee was safe from Maydet's men. They could raid at will, safe in the knowledge that Midland wouldn't move against them.

"I'll want both horses, Hutch," Will said stubbornly. "They're both beat, but I can spell them."

"You're still going?"

Will said flatly, almost angrily, "If I don't go, I might as well quit."

"Then let me go with you."

Anger flared in Gannon's eyes. "Damn it, Hutch, we're running a stage line! That's the only reason I'm here or you're here. That comes first, always."

He did not wait for Hutch to answer, but moved over to Keefe's grub box. There he found a sack and filled it with the jerky and cold biscuits that Keefe had made from the new provisions. Then, leaving the shack, he went out to the barn and partially filled a gunny sack with grain which he flattened out, rolled up, and tied behind the blanket roll on his waiting horse.

Hutch took the saddle and bridle off his horse, put on a lead rope, and stood watching from the door, the sting of Gannon's reproof still showing in his face. Gannon stepped into the saddle and the two men regarded each other.

"How long do I wait, Will?" Hutch asked.

Gannon knew he was asking how long he should wait before he followed him, but Will purposely misunderstood him. "Until I get back," he said flatly and pulled his horses around.

The tracks of the driven horse herd were as plain

as a printed page as they headed south and west across the prairie aiming toward the mountains to the south. Gannon let his tired horse make its own pace. Twice at buffalo wallows he let his horses drink just as the drivers of the stolen herd had let the herd drink.

When darkness fell, he was in the shallow foothills. Here he grained his horses and let them graze for an hour while he ate a cold supper and speculated on what lay ahead.

Long before darkness had set in he had examined the country to the west with close attention. The foothills thrust out into the prairie from the mountains like fingers extended from a hand and the herd had aimed between the two low ridges where he was now resting. In all probability the two ridges would lift as he traveled west, and what was a shallow dip here would become a canyon farther on. Up there somewhere they would be waiting for him, probably with a guard staked out to warn them of his coming and to seal off his escape. They would be careful enough to figure he might travel by night and would accordingly be ready for that too.

When Will saddled Hutch's fresher horse and picketed his own, he knew what he was going to do. Tonight he would travel, but not up this beginning canyon. He would cross the ridge to the south, traveling the next canyon, paralleling the trail of the stolen horses. He could only hope that they would keep to the canyon they had entered. Just before daylight he could cross over and at first light confirm that the herd had passed by. It would be possible then to travel the ridge and move on.

He moved over into the next canyon and set himself to conserve his horse's strength. As he traveled on and the canyon walls became higher and began to narrow, Will wondered what lay ahead of him. Hutch's reasoning was probably correct, for in reading the signs left by the herd he could see no indication that their drivers had been in a hurry. They had watered the horses at every opportunity and once had let them graze. Thieves concerned with pursuit and capture would have pushed the herd mercilessly, putting hope of escape in distance and a change of weather that would blot out sign. Since these men had been in no hurry, it meant they were expecting and would welcome pursuit to a place where they had previously elected to stand.

Before false dawn, Will pulled his tired horse up the north ridge which held a thick stand of timber and put him down the other side. Just before daylight came, he confirmed by shielded matchlight that the horses had passed here, holding west for the deep mountains. Before real daylight he was back in the screening timber of the ridge. Now he warily traveled the ridge, keeping to the timber, only occasionally pulling over to the rim to see what the coming morning would reveal.

It was on one of these careful excursions to the edge of the timber that he caught a glimpse of a meadow ahead where the far canyon rim to the north fell back. His curiosity heightened, he pulled back into the timber and pushed on, and when he judged he was opposite the meadow he reined in, dismounted, and moved over to the edge of the timber. There below him lay a wide meadow of wild hay; the Dry Creek horses were loosely bunched and grazing at its upper end. As he was watching, feeling his heart pounding, he saw a faint streamer of smoke rising from the trees at the east end of the meadow.

Moving swiftly along the rim, Will reached a spot where he could see through the trees to the source of the smoke. It was a small log cabin with thin beginning smoke coming out of its rock and mud chimney.

For several minutes Will regarded the cabin, and when he had a clear view of the cabin and the ground around it, he felt his heart begin to pound with excitement. There was no corral in sight. Whoever was in the cabin had turned their horses loose to graze with the herd.

Now Will rose and ran back to his horse and mounted swiftly. Still clinging to the timber, he pushed on west, and presently, when he judged he was at the end of the meadow, he pulled off the rim and gained the valley floor. Turning east through the timber, he came to the edge of the meadow and halted for only a moment. He thought bleakly, *This is chancy,* and wondered if his horse had the bottom to make it. If he had, Will knew he could leave these men afoot.

He saw one of the grazing horses lift his head, ears alert, and heard him snort uneasily. Will knew that he could wait no longer. Drawing a deep breath into his lungs, he let out a scream of a mountain lion and savagely roweled his horse through the trees, heading for the meadow. When he broke out of the timber at a dead run, the grazing horses were already panicked and in motion and Will tried desperately to close the gap between himself and the herd. Three horses at the north edge of the timber were running tardily for the protection of the herd and now Will's horse was amongst them.

He glanced ahead at the cabin and saw three men boil out of it; two were waving their arms, guns in hand, while the third was waving a coat as he let off a rifle in an effort to turn the oncoming horses.

Will lifted out his gun, grabbed the mane of his laboring horse with his gun hand, kicked his left foot free of the stirrup and, Indian fashion, swung down alongside his horse's neck, his leg under the horse's belly. Then he shot and whistled piercingly.

The terrified horses, at full gallop, were strung out in a stampeding line. Will's horse was toward the rear, with the herd between it and the men from the shack. He heard shots now as he came almost abreast of the men and he heard two horses scream and go down. The lead horse severed away from the men but did not even slow.

Now he was abreast of the men and, looking under his horse's neck, he saw that the man with the rifle was Richie Cleff. He was shooting blindly into the herd as it galloped past him and down canyon. Will heard a horse behind him go down with a savage grunt, and then they were past the cabin.

Still keeping down, he looked back and saw four horses struggling in the meadow. Cleff was still shooting, while the other two men were chasing a limping horse.

Then he was in the narrowing canyon and he reined in his almost foundered pony. There was a patch of timber ahead that the still stampeding herd skirted at full gallop. Will put his horse into the timber and dismounted, pulling his rifle from its scabbard. He led his horse deeper into the timber and then came back to the edge of the clearing. Squatting now against a tree, he waited, a grim elation riding him as the clatter of the stampeding horses faded and almost died.

There would be a guard below somewhere and he would have been alerted by the gunfire. Whether he would try to stop the stampeding horses or return to discover the reason for the shooting, Will didn't know. He waited, listening to the now still morning in which the only sound was bird song.

Presently he picked up the sound of a horse approaching at full gallop and he lifted his rifle. Suddenly the horseman rounded the edge of the timber and Will saw the gun in his hand. Immediately the horseman saw Will and snapped a shot, reining his horse abruptly to the left and rearing him. Will sighted on the horse's chest and waited until the horse came down on all fours, bringing the man's shirt into Will's sight. He fired, and saw the man wiped out of the saddle as if by a giant hand.

Now Will rose, his legs driving under him as he raced to cut off the frightened horse. Yelling, he waved his hat and whistled shrilly. The horse shied away from him, turned, and cut back down canyon at a dead run. Will stood there, hat in one hand, rifle in the other, and dragged deep gusts of the morning air into his aching lungs. Beyond the dead weariness in him rode a wild elation. Cleff and his crew were afoot and their companion dead, and the horse herd was on its way back to Dry Creek, safe from any pursuit.

4

The passengers of the eastbound were stirring around the common room, some of them paying Mrs. Lennor their fifty cents for the meal just finished and some idling about the porch watching Lennor across the road doping the axles of their coach in the midday sunshine.

Carrie Bentall came in from the kitchen with a wedge of pie on a plate which she set down for Wilsey Kirk, the driver, the last diner to finish.

Wilsey wiped his mouth and beard with a lifted sweep of his forearm and shook his head. "Can't do it, Carrie, but that meal sure made up for Boley's."

"I thought that was going to be changed," Carrie said.

" 'Tis some," Wilsey conceded. "It's cleaner, but the food's no different. He's got to scare 'em again."

"Gannon, you mean," Carrie said quietly.

Wilsey looked up at her and nodded. "How's Keefe?"

Carrie sank onto the bench, glad for this small break. An involuntary sigh escaped her. "He's eating a little. Mostly though he's out of his head with fever."

"You look like you been nursing him," Wilsey said in a quiet tone.

Carrie smiled faintly and nodded.

"Can I talk with him?"

"He's sleeping now. I don't think you'd better."

"Then cheer him up with this news when he wakes up," Wilsey said. "Gannon tracked the bunch down that shot Keefe. He killed one, set the rest of 'em afoot eighty miles from the closest horse, and got his horses back."

Carrie said, almost without interest, "I'll tell him."

Wilsey's pale eyes regarded Carrie with shrewdness. "What's the matter? Has he scorched you, too?"

Carrie shook her head. "There's no reason to, but that doesn't mean he won't."

"That's a fact," Wilsey agreed soberly. "He don't care who he rakes over, not even his best friend."

Carrie frowned. "Hutch, you mean?"

Wilsey nodded. "Hutch was at Boley's when I come through last night and he rode with me down to Dry Creek. Gannon had got back with the horses sometime in the night. Seems he'd left Hutch to tend the station. Hutch had changed horses for the westbound, rode up to Boley's with it, and came back with me, so he was always there to make the team change. That didn't suit Gannon though." Wilsey shook his head, as if remembering. "Hutch no sooner hit the ground than Gannon lit on him. Hutch took a raking like I never heard a man take before. I thought there'd be gunplay."

Carrie shook her head. "No, Hutch is scared of him," Carrie said, an odd bitterness in her voice. "Everybody's scared of him. That's what he wants."

"Well, he's a rough man," Wilsey said reflectively. "You know what he told me when I pulled out?"

Carrie waited.

"He said, 'Tell everyone down the line that I got our horses back, Wilsey. Tell 'em I killed a man to do it. Tell 'em that squares things up for Keefe. Tell 'em Midland takes care of its own people.' " Wilsey paused. "Yes, he's rough."

"You like it that way, Wilsey?" Carrie asked quietly.

Wilsey thought a moment, gently scratching his chin through his beard. "I reckon I do," he said at last. "A man's going to think twice before he stops my stage, points a gun at me, and tells me to throw down the loot. He'll know he's got Gannon on his neck and that Gannon won't quit till he gets him."

"And the other drivers feel that way too?"

"Mostly." He was watching Carrie and he said abruptly, "You don't like him."

Carrie stood up and said, with scarcely an inflection in her voice, "I don't feel any way about him, Wilsey. I don't even work for him."

Wilsey put both hands on the table, as if to rise. "Well, he ain't a happy man, that's for sure," Wilsey said. Then, as if remembering something, he added, "What I brought him today didn't make him any happier."

Carrie waited, curious.

Wilsey shrugged and stood up. "Kirby give me a hand-passed letter for him from Salt Lake. When he read it he just walked away from the team change, but he looked like somebody'd kicked him in the belly." Wilsey looked at her. "What do you figure?"

"I don't, Wilsey," Carrie said. She began to gather up the dishes. "People get bad news all the time."

"Not all the time, Carrie, just most of the time," Wilsey said drily. He smiled at her, picked up his elbow-length gauntlets, and went out.

Carrie went about her business clearing off the table and presently Mrs. Lennor came out into the kitchen to help her with the dishes. They did not talk and it seemed to Carrie that long since they had used up all subjects for conversation. When they were finished, Mrs. Lennor said, "I'll go sit with Keefe a spell, and you take a rest."

Carrie nodded and Mrs. Lennor stepped out the back door and crossed to the bunkhouse where Keefe had been put. The women watched him during the day and Lennor or the stocktender watched him during the night. Carrie sometimes wondered, watching his suffering, if it wouldn't have been more merciful if the bullet had killed him.

She hung the dish towels above the stove to dry and then moved into the common room to see that all was in order. Glancing through the open door, she saw that the stage was long gone and that a pair of ox-drawn immigrant wagons was halted in the road, their menfolk talking with Lennor. The chunking sound of an axe biting deep into timber of the new barn beyond the wagons was the only sound in the afternoon.

She would have liked to sit down for a moment, but she knew that Mrs. Lennor expected her to do the weekly chore of airing the bunkhouse blankets.

When she stepped into the bunkhouse, Mrs. Lennor was seated in a rocking chair at the far end of the big room. The blanket which curtained off Keefe's bunk was pulled halfway to allow air to circulate. Mrs. Lennor did not speak but watched Carrie as she folded blankets and took them in her arms. Once outside, Carrie turned west, heading out over the green prairie. The faint breeze with its smell of spring teased at her skirt and stirred her hair.

A hundred yards from the bunkhouse was a series of mounded anthills. Carrie approached them and then put her burden on the grass. Unfolding a blanket, she spread it on the first anthill and then walked across it to disturb the red ants. Returning to the pile of blankets, she picked up another one and spread it on a second anthill, and did the same with the third and fourth blankets.

Turning back to the bunkhouse for her second trip, she wondered if Keefe would be in any condition to understand Wilsey's news or if he even cared whether his shooting was revenged or not. It seemed to her that the news of revenge was becoming too common lately and that it was always associated with Will Gannon. First he had killed a man for burning Lennor's barn. Now he had killed another man for stealing horses. She supposed it was true that a man must defend his own property and that in a lawless country this sometimes meant killing, but she was weary of this news of violence that each driver brought to their isolated station.

Each time it made her wonder what kind of a man Gannon really was. It seemed to her that he must like violence for the sake of violence. Else why was there always this feeling of physical threat in the background when men talked about him? It was even there when Wilsey acknowledged it was comforting to know a man would think twice before holding up a stage because of the knowledge that the implacable Gannon would be on his trail.

Carrie saw the two immigrant wagons pull out, their conversation with Lennor finished. Watching the plodding oxen, their drivers tramping beside them, Carrie wondered where they were going and what the future held for them. And this made her remember that once she too had been headed west with hope for a bright future. Instead she had found this cheerless haven which she privately thought of as a kind of purgatory. She worked out the hours of the day and slept out the hours of the night, but nothing really ever happened. The past was dimming and there was no future, just the too ordinary present.

She got her second load of blankets and as she was walking toward the anthills, she saw a lone rider approaching from the west. She noted he had stopped to talk with the ox drivers, and then she busied herself spreading out the blankets on the anthills. She had just finished her chore and was counting the blankets when she heard a horse approaching. Finishing her count, she turned and saw that it was Will Gannon who had reined up beside her. His gaunt features were blurred by black beard stubble and there was a deadly soberness in his eyes that made Carrie want to look away.

He touched his hat and asked, "How's Keefe doing?"

Carrie told him, adding, "He may be awake by now. He's in the bunkhouse."

Gannon accepted this in silence, and Carrie, watching him, thought, *He's not even listening. Something's wrong.* She found herself almost unwilling to talk with him, and she turned and walked across the last blankets she had laid down. Gannon, she knew, was watching her and when she was finished she looked up at him.

"What's that you're doing?" he asked, and pulled his horse over to her. For a moment, Carrie saw, curiosity had replaced the sickness in his eyes.

Carrie smiled faintly. "All your stage passengers aren't the cleanest people in the world, Mr. Gannon. They bring lice with them and leave them on the blankets. Once a week we spread the blankets on these hills of red ants. Tomorrow when I pick up the blankets the red ants will have cleaned them of lice."

As she finished talking Carrie saw that the interest in Gannon's eyes had vanished and the old sickness was there. He dismounted and together they headed toward the house, Will leading his horse and making no effort at conversation. Was it remorse she was watching work in him, Carrie wondered. Had he seen himself for the bully he was?

Suddenly she remembered Wilsey's words describing Gannon's reactions to the letter passed him by Wilsey. *He looked like he'd been kicked in the belly.* That was it then, Carrie thought. Some bad news had put a dismal burden upon him, and she wondered what it could be. She realized then that she knew nothing about this man save that he had been a division agent farther west on the Midland. A friendlier man would long since have told something of himself, of what he had been and seen and done. In a different way, she thought, Gannon was like the tough riffraff who drifted past Lennor's and stopped for a meal—secretive, watchful, without visible ties and without any history at all.

She saw him watching the stocktender and Lennor as they wrestled with the drop logs of the new barn, and there was only indifference in his face. At the bunkhouse they parted without speaking and Carrie felt a small hope die that she had never known existed. Whatever she had thought of Gannon before, she had known that, unlike the Lennors, he was not indifferent to her existence, and because of that there had been a kind of excitement in their meetings. That was gone now, she knew; like the Lennors, he had put her aside for his own private thoughts. She had never felt more lonely.

Will dropped his reins and turned into the bunkhouse. He saw that the two bunks at the end had been curtained off with a blanket, and Mrs. Lennor, her feet firmly planted on the floor, sat in a rocking chair knitting. At his entrance she greeted him unsmilingly and folded the knitting in her lap.

"Is he awake, Mrs. Lennor?"

"He was a while ago, Mr. Gannon. I fed him some broth and he went to sleep right afterwards."

Will moved across the room and drew back the curtain. The first thing he noticed about Keefe was that there was some color in his cheeks. He was stripped to the waist and Gannon could see a clean bandage on his side.

Gannon said, "I'll watch him if you want to do something else."

Mrs. Lennor rose and said, matter-of-factly, "I could be doing some things."

Will nodded and watched her go out. Then he moved to one of the bunks and sat down, over-

whelmed by weariness. Slowly then it crept back
into his mind and his hand started almost instinc-
tively for his shirt pocket. *It said it,* he thought;
there's no use reading it again or carrying it around.
His hand moved on as he came to his decision. He
took out the envelope and fumbled in his coat
pocket for a match. Extracting a piece of paper from
the envelope, he read its message, struck the match,
lit paper and envelope, and dropped them to the dirt
floor, watching the brief flames consume them. Now
he took off his hat and lay back in the bunk. It was
all right now. The disbelief was ended, now that the
note was burned. After the fiftieth reading he had
accepted its message, which he could have memorized, and did, on first reading. It had said, "Just
learned from San Francisco that Mrs. Gannon is
dead by her own hand. Thought you'd want to
know. Blayne."

Blayne, Salt Lake division agent for the line, and
his good friend, had been kind enough and at the
same time cruel enough to put on paper what he
would have inevitably heard, and now it was finished.

There was no use running from it any longer or
tiring himself to exhaustion, or even thinking about
it. Marian was dead.

When Wilsey had given him the letter and he had
read it, he had never known such immediate, crush-
ing punishment. Like a sick animal, his instinct had
been to get away from his kind, and he had saddled
up and ridden away from Hutch. All this day reason
kept repeating, *You'd lost her anyway. What does it
matter if she's dead?* But that didn't lessen the anguish. Had she taken her life because of her feeling

of guilt over deserting him? Or had she found life intolerable with her new man? He would never know and he really didn't want to know. All he knew now was that he had loved her beyond his own understanding and that, without ever putting it into framed thought, he had planned, when he had swallowed his hard pride, to get her back. All of it, the love, the hurt, the anger, and the pride, both the sweet and the bitter memories had all been senseless; none of it had amounted to a damn, and nothing ever would be worth a damn again.

He slept, and it was the sleep of physical and spiritual exhaustion. An idle breeze stirring through the open door presently scattered the ashes of the letter across the floor until no trace of it remained.

The return of the stocktenders from their work on the barn wakened him, and he was immediately aware of the feeling of guilt that Keefe was moaning in fever behind the curtain. Gannon went up to the house to report it and Carrie left immediately for the bunk room, while Gannon, feeling helpless and guilty, watched her go. Then, to be doing something, he asked Lennor for the loan of his razor, borrowed a basin of hot water from the stove, and shaved and washed at the bench beside the back door in the fading evening light.

At supper, which they ate in the common room because of their numbers, Gannon picked up the gossip of the line. Olderson had stopped by on his way west, leaving word with Lennor for Gannon that an emergency in one of the western divisions made it imperative for him to leave. Maydet's inventory was completed and in the hands of young Dickert, who seemed capable of handling the office work. Olderson had bought some of the needed horses and had two reasonably reliable men out buying feed. But the division badly needed an agent, someone with more authority and years than Dickert, who could bring some semblance of order to the Louisburg end.

Will listened to Lennor and knew that he would have to do something immediately about a new division agent and he knew it could not be Hutch. The first responsibility he had given Hutch—the keeping of the Dry Creek Station—had resulted in Hutch failing him. Hutch's reasons for his dereliction were not good enough. Hutch had claimed that no stage had missed a team change while Will had gone after the stolen herd, and that since Gannon had directed Boley to clean up his place, it was perfectly proper for Hutch to check on Boley. Still, Hutch should have known that he was leaving the station open to plundering and the six horses from the team change open to theft. No, Hutch was not his man.

Gannon noticed that Carrie did not appear during supper, and when they had left the table, Gannon went back to the bunkhouse. She was feeding Keefe when he entered and he moved over to Keefe's bunk. The youngster smiled wanly at him through fever-cracked lips and they shook hands.

Gannon saw the shadow of pain still lingering in the boy's eyes, but he also saw that Keefe had learned to conquer that pain.

"Carrie says you got 'em back," Keefe said.

Gannon nodded. "We did a little more than that."

"Oh?" Keefe asked, and looked inquiringly at Carrie.

"One man killed and the rest set afoot," Carrie said tonelessly.

"You didn't tell me that," Keefe said.

"No," Carrie said, and left it there. She held a spoonful of broth up to Keefe's mouth but he shook his head.

"I'd just like to sleep again," Keefe said apologetically.

"You do that," Gannon said. "We'll be around."

As Carrie put away Keefe's dishes and began to tidy up his bunk, Gannon moved out into the night and halted. It was odd, he thought, that Carrie should have told Keefe of the recovery of the horses without telling him the rest of it. Now as he packed his pipe and lighted it, he saw his saddle and blanket roll against the bunkhouse wall, and he was suddenly aware that while he had slept someone had taken care of his horse. He heard a sound behind him, turned, and saw Carrie's silhouette in the bunkhouse doorway before she stepped through and brushed past him on the way to the house.

"Carrie," Will called, and heard her halt in the darkness. He came up to her and asked, "How do you think he is?"

"I don't know," Carrie said. "He eats and sleeps. That can't be anything but good, can it?"

"No. But you thought my news would upset him?" He put the question tentatively, as if puzzled.

"About the killing, you mean?"

"Yes."

"I guess I didn't want to tell him," Carrie said quietly. She paused. "If you want to make a habit of greeting people by saying, 'Hello, I just killed a man yesterday,' that's your business."

She did not wait for him to comment but went on into the house.

The surprised protest that Will framed never left his lips: he would have been talking to her back in the darkness. An angry puzzlement came to him now as he watched her step through the back door. Was she reproving him for having shot a man who was shooting at him? Or was she trying to withhold knowledge from Keefe that would disturb him? Gannon thought of Keefe, young, but far older than his years, more than willing to give better than he took from riffraff, Indians, or Maydet's bully boys. Still, Carrie's words disturbed him and he moved idly out into the night, thinking about the girl.

He strolled across the road, catching the resin scent of the newly cut barn logs, and moved past stacked timbers to the repaired corral. Then, on impulse, he turned, wanting to see Carrie and get her explanation. Better let the Lennors get out of the way first, he thought. He leaned on the top rail of the corral, smoking, and waited patiently until he saw Mrs. Lennor close and bolt the porch door and take the lamp upstairs to her bedroom. Carrie, he supposed, would be eating the supper she had missed, and he crossed the road, circled the house, and came in the rear door. His guess had been right; Carrie, seated alone at the kitchen table, was finishing her supper. Gannon was abruptly conscious of both the loneliness and self-sufficiency of this quiet girl.

He moved over to the stove, picked up the coffee pot, crossed the room, filled Carrie's cup and the cup beside a place already set out for the morning. Then he slacked into a chair facing Carrie and in silence drank his coffee, watching her finish her piece of pie. She was not embarrassed and seemed unconcerned about his presence, Will thought, and he recalled her strange words outside the bunkhouse.

When she leaned back in her chair and lifted her glance to him, Gannon smiled faintly. "Something about me is bothering you, Carrie," he said. "What is it?"

Carrie shook her head and looked directly into his eyes. "It doesn't matter, and you wouldn't want to hear it."

"I want to."

Carrie said nothing, and was not about to say anything, he saw.

He asked quietly, "Have I ever said to you, 'Hello, I killed a man yesterday'?"

"No, I was exaggerating."

"But why were you?" Gannon pushed.

"That's just the way it seems to us here," Carrie said calmly. "We get news of everything you do. You slap a man at this station, you curse a man and threaten to replace him at the next station. You shoot a man at another station for trying to steal your horses, and you let other people bury him. When someone really does steal your horses you kill him. Maybe that's all necessary. I don't know. But then you tell the drivers, 'Pass the news down the line about how tough I am.'"

Gannon felt his face flush. "For a reason, Carrie," he said.

"I know," Carrie said drily. "You want to scare the bad ones off, scare the lazy ones into work, and scare the good ones into being better."

"That's an odd way of saying a man wants to do a good job."

"It may be odd, but it's true," Carrie said quietly. "Have I scared you?"

Carrie looked thoughtful, the dark wings of her eyebrows drawn together, but she still regarded him evenly. "I suppose you have," she said then. "Not directly. Still, you scare me into not liking you very much, and I like to like people."

"How have I scared you?" Will demanded.

"Like that," Carrie said swiftly. "Pushing me into a corner, demanding why I feel the way I do, making me say things I'd never say if you didn't ask them."

It was Will's turn to be silent, for there was no answering her reproof.

Presently Carrie said, "I told you you wouldn't like it."

Will shifted in his chair, uncomfortable under her quiet gaze and surprised at the lack of passion in her speech. He couldn't help but remember that Marian used to come at him with fury in an argument, so that he would have to wait out her raging torrent of abuse before peace was achieved. Now he made an effort to recall the other times he had talked with Carrie. At their first meeting when he had baited her over the neglected mail bags, he knew he had been abrupt and irritated. Too, his nerves were still raw with the memory of Marian, just as they had been the second time they met here, but he felt no impatience with her now and was making this effort to be friendly. Had he been dealing with shirkers and malingerers so long that his roughness toward them had spilled over into his relations with her? He didn't think so. She had simply misunderstood his need to discipline the slack people under him and to defend, at the point of a gun, the property that was entrusted to him.

He said, almost with impatience, "How would you have me be, Carrie?"

She rose and said calmly, "Gentler," and picked up her plate and cup, moving toward the dishpan on the stove.

"I'll remember that," Will said drily, almost angrily. "When I'm dealing with Maydet or these riff-raff horse thieves, I'll try to remember I should turn the other cheek. But I won't do it, Carrie, and you know why."

"You must have a good reason why you won't," she said quietly.

"I have. I'd get my head belted off my neck."

Carrie half turned and looked at him. "You don't know it, but you will anyway."

Will scowled. "Now what does that mean?"

Carrie only shook her head. "You're so sure of yourself," she murmured. "Sure people are always wrong. You can't afford to be wrong because you've enforced your judgment with violence. Once you're wrong, violence catches up with you, doesn't it?"

Gannon rose now and said drily, thinking to trap her, "You're sure you're right about that?"

Carrie looked at him swiftly. "No. I just have a feeling."

"Good night," Will said, and moved out into the night, hearing her quiet "Good night, Will." He was out the back door and onto the hard-packed dirt before he hauled up, realizing that she had called him Will. She had said it freely and almost with pity in the tone of her voice. Then he slowly moved toward the bunkhouse, wondering at this girl. Her talk, the very meaning of her words, was elusive. She would have him gentler, less sure of himself, else he would die by violence. A wry amusement touched him now as he thought of the job ahead of him and the men whose enmity he was earning. Only a pleasantly daft, solitary girl, gentle as a woman should be, could seriously give this advice. But the hint of pity in her good night disturbed him still as he stepped into the bunkhouse.

He looked in on Keefe, saw that he was sleeping, turned down the lamp on the table, and rolled into the closest empty bunk.

Gannon made Louisburg late the following night, slept in the hotel, had an early breakfast in the hotel dining room filled with departing travelers, and stepped out into the street. The town was already astir and the new sun laid long shadows to the west of all that moved and stood.

Will crossed the wide hard-packed road to Maydet's log store and stepped inside. To the right he saw young Dickert making change for stage fare for two waiting passengers. Will crossed over and stood by the rail till Dickert concluded his business and said to the two men, "Have a good trip." Then he turned to Will, saying, "Yes sir, what— Why, Mr. Gannon!"

"How are you, Bert?" Will said, and they shook hands. "How's it going?"

Young Dickert ran a hand through his blond hair and grinned. "Well, we're making money."

"That's the idea," Will said, and stepped inside the enclosure.

Dickert waited politely until Will sat down in the straight-back chair before the desk and then he began to talk stage business. As Will listened, answering questions, nodding approval, and making suggestions, he watched young Dickert. Sudden responsibility had matured Bert, he decided. He spoke quietly, but with authority and knowledge of his job. Will learned that upon receiving Wilsey's news of the return of the stolen herd to Dry Creek, Bert had dispatched a second messenger coach to clean up the last of the backed-up mail in the division stations. The accounts were in order, Bert said, but he could not answer for the maintenance or the feed buying. All he knew was that the head stocktender was receiving wild hay from over east and oats and corn from the railhead to the north, and that he had managed so far to come up with enough teams to send off every coach, including the messenger, on schedule.

When Bert had brought the account of his work up to date, Will leaned back in his chair. "Have you picked up anything, Bert, that might tell us who killed your uncle?"

Bert's eyes altered subtly into hardness. "Nothing I can put my finger on, Mr. Gannon, but I don't have to look far."

"No farther than this store?"

Bert nodded. "I watch every night," Bert said grimly. "Not a night goes by but what some traveler isn't roughed up and robbed. When the local people aren't sitting in the games over at the saloon, they're crooked. Maydet owns the saloon and hires the dealers. The crew that hangs around him never does any work, but they always have money. I don't think it's theirs."

Will glanced beyond Bert and saw Maydet coming up an aisle of the store, his burly body rolling from side to side as he walked. He was freshly shaven and his half-circle dark mustache was newly trimmed over his thick pouting lips. The knife scar on his cheek showed plainly, and he seemed to wear it with arrogance. His hooded eyes saw Gannon and his glance slid away as he halted by a clerk and spoke to him.

"We'll talk about that later, Bert," Gannon murmured, and rose. Moving out of the enclosure, he walked toward Maydet, whose massive body bulked over the clerk. At Gannon's approach, Maydet turned his head, then dipped it in a nod, saying, "Back home at last, are you, Gannon?"

Will halted and regarded him. "I saw some friends of yours a few days ago."

Maydet's black brows lifted in inquiry. "Well, I have a lot of 'em. Who was it?"

"Richie Cleff and three others."

"That no-good," Maydet said. "Where'd you see him?"

"With about eighteen of my horses," Will said, watching him.

The blandness on Maydet's big face altered into momentary puzzlement, then he said, "Oh, I heard about that. Was Cleff running with that gang?"

"Running with it, or running it, I didn't stop to ask."

Maydet shook his head. "He's wild, that lad is. That's why I run him out of here."

"When was this?"

"Some days ago," Maydet said idly. "He sat in for a sick dealer over at the saloon. Damned if I didn't catch him using marked cards. I threw him out."

Gannon had to admire the man. He probably knew that Dickert had spotted the crooked games and was now admitting to them by disclaiming Cleff. Will knew there was no way he could tie Cleff to Maydet so long as Maydet disclaimed him.

"Speaking of horses, I want a word with you," Maydet said. "Let's go back to the office."

Will nodded. Maydet turned and walked down the aisle toward the rear of the store, his rolling body reminding Will of a walking bear. Maydet entered a cubbyhole of a room holding a littered flat-top desk and a big safe whose doors were closed. A high, unwashed window to the right of the desk let in a pale light that would be at Maydet's back when he sat at his desk. Maydet gestured to the straight chair against the wall beside the desk, while he himself slacked into the padded swivel chair before the desk. The chair creaked under his massive weight.

Will sat down, and Maydet, swearing under his breath, rose, reached in his pocket for his knife. He opened the blade, picked up a plug of tobacco from his desk, cut off a wedge of the plug, and extended the knife to Will with a piece of plug held between the blade and thumb. When Will shook his head, Maydet lifted the piece of tobacco to his mouth, delicately licked both sides of the blade, then closed the knife.

"This happened when I was division agent, but it don't concern me now. I just thought I'd tell you," Maydet began. "Remember those horses that were run off from Dry Creek Station when I was division agent?"

Will nodded.

Maydet, toying with the knife, held it up and looked at it, then his glance shuttled lazily to Will. "I had a man come to me and ask if I wanted to buy them back. I told him I'd ask you."

Will leaned forward. "Buy them back?" he murmured.

Maydet inclined his head. "It happened all the time to me when I was division agent."

"You mean this man steals your horses, then comes and asks you to buy them back?"

Maydet leaned over and spit between his legs. "Oh, not the same man that stole them," Maydet said mildly. "Hell, if it was the same man, I'd shoot him. No, it isn't worked like that."

"How is it worked?" Will asked thinly.

"You know how it is," Maydet said, his voice matter-of-fact and friendly. "These damn roughs will sneak in on a station and drive off the horses. Sometimes they're Injuns, sometimes they're breeds, and sometimes they're whites living with Injuns or breeds. If a man's got a station to hold down, he can't go chasing horses. Even if he does, this country's a mighty big place. They can't cover it all. Well, what happens?"

"Tell me," Will said.

"You just wait a while and one day a man comes in and asks you if you want to buy some horses. You always want to buy horses. So you go out and take a look at them. They're your horses, but the brand's been changed. The man has a bill of sale and the horses are cheap. The second time this man comes around you don't bother to look at the horses. They're yours, but he's got proof they're his. You just buy them back."

"You don't do anything to the man who holds a crooked bill of sale?"

Maydet's massive shoulders lifted. "You still don't see it. He didn't steal the horses and likely he don't know who did. He's got a good bill of sale and likely the man before him had, so it's all legal. The thieves know and you know those are your horses. They also know that the nearest law is a couple of hundred miles away. Are you going to law and months of court fighting when it's easier to buy back your horses cheap?"

"I'd track down the party who gave the bill of sale."

Maydet shook his head. "The man's gone west, moved out, or he's gone east."

"If the seller is giving you cheap horses, he knows they're stolen, doesn't he?"

Maydet snorted, "Of course he does. But he didn't steal them. His cousin or a cousin of a cousin did. He's just the go-between and you've got nothing on him."

Gannon tried to keep his face impassive, but he could feel a vein in his neck pulsing with anger. With bland gall, Maydet was offering to sell him back the horses Maydet himself had stolen. He was even claiming that he had followed this practice when he was the division agent and he was probably telling the truth, Will thought grimly. Maydet, as division agent, very likely had his own men steal his horses, then spent company money to buy them back, explaining that while he was dealing with thieves he could not get proof and that it was cheaper than legally prosecuting them.

Will lazily crossed his legs, trying to keep suspicion and anger from showing in his face. "I see your point," he conceded mildly. "It's cheaper to deal than to try and track down ownership."

Again Maydet inclined his head. "I always figured it was when I was division agent. You can suit yourself."

"How many has your seller got and what does he want for them?"

"Fifteen at five dollars a head," Maydet said calmly.

"That's cheap enough. When can he deliver?"

"Tonight," Maydet said. "You pay me the money and I'll hold it. The horses will be left in the corral sometime tonight. Look them over tomorrow and if the count's right, I'll pass on the money."

Gannon stood up. "I'll tell Dickert to give you the money. You might pass on a message to the man you give it to."

"All right."

"Tell him the next time we have some horses stolen I'll get them back if I have to go to California to do it."

He saw the amused malice in Maydet's eyes, but the big man's face was bland. "I'll tell him," he said.

Will nodded and tramped out, wondering if Maydet had noticed his suppressed wrath, wondering too if Maydet really thought him that gullible. Will hoped his pretense of accepting Maydet's suggestion that he buy the horses had been convincing enough, for it was only pretense.

He paused at the enclosure long enough to instruct Dickert to pay over seventy-five dollars to Maydet for horses. As he was turning away, Dickert said, "Just a minute, Mr. Gannon."

He reached in a pigeonhole of the desk and brought out a piece of paper which he handed to Will, saying, "From Mr. Olderson."

Will unfolded the paper and read: "Will, Union Pacific informs me a specie shipment of $60,000 is due at end of steel, around the 27th, to be laid down here. This should give you time to pull in reliable guards from the western divisions in case you mistrust what men are available here, Olderson."

The 27th was six days away, and Will, grimly acknowledging that there were no reliable guards available, made a mental note to send word by tomorrow's stage to Blayne in Salt Lake City.

He spent the rest of the day in the shops, barns, and stables doing the chores of the nonexistent division agent. Hugh Kelly, the man Hutch had recommended as the best man for division agent, was a driver and was out on a run. Until he returned and Will talked with him, Will knew he must handle the division affairs himself. But at one time during that busy day Will took time to reconnoiter the buildings around the big corral where the horses would be delivered that night. A big feed barn adjoined it and Will prowled its lower floor. There was a small room opening onto the corral at one corner of the barn and when Will opened the door the rank smell of tar and liniment came to him. Looking inside, he saw ranks of jugged medicines and veterinary tools hanging from nails on the wall. He noted also that there was an entrance door from the barn's interior.

That evening Will had supper with Bert Dickert

and parted from him at dark, heading back through the idling street crowds to the shops. Rufe was in the filthy stable office when Will entered and halted, looking around him at the dust-covered sagging desk littered with straps of harness, at the cracked leather sofa with one leg missing, and finally at the board on the wall holding tagged keys.

"My horse has a cut," Will said. "Got a key to the vet's cupboard?"

Rufe moved over to the key board, saying, "You'll want the key to the feed barn. You can get to it through there." He lifted down a key and Will accepted it, thanking him.

At full dark Will let himself into the feed barn and walked its length, listening to the whispering scurry of the mice and rats. Once in the vet's cupboard, Will moved to the corral door, unbolted it, and opened it wide enough so that he could dimly make out the corral gate. Then he fumbled around, found a block of wood which the vet used as a stepladder to reach his highest shelf, placed it before the door, and sat down. Maydet might have been satisfied that the men who delivered the horses were not a party to the theft, but Will was not. They would either talk or pay the penalty of silence.

Will supposed by the diminished sounds of the town that it was close to midnight when he heard the hoof beats of moving horses. Presently he could make out the dim form of a rider approaching the corral gate. He saw the man attempt to open the gate from horseback, heard him swear, then dismount and push open the gate, leading his horse inside. In a moment the horses entered the corral, a second rider hazing them from the rear with shrill whistles.

Silently Will pushed the door open and stepped out into the night, lifting his gun from its holster. He moved swiftly now toward the dismounted man and then called sharply, "Hold on there!"

As he spoke an orange flare and the racketing shot of a pistol boomed out from the corner of the barn to his left. Will half turned and shot blindly at the flame, knowing as he did so that he should not have returned the fire but should have dropped to the ground.

And then the big sound came and a tearing agony slammed at his back and side, knocking him flat on his face into the dirt of the corral. He knew without even framing it in his mind that a man had been waiting at the cupboard corner of the barn with a shotgun to shoot him in the back. He had walked into Maydet's trap.

In those terrible seconds while he struggled to replace the air driven from his lungs, he was certain he was going to die. With a massive effort that engulfed him in pain, he rolled over, shot toward the corner of the barn, and then was wretchedly aware that men and horses were running, whether at him or away from him he did not know, for he was drowning in an ocean of pain.

5

Yet he never quite lost consciousness. As the panicked horses thundered over him and around him, he lay gagging, breathing the choking dust into his lungs as he fought for air, knowing somehow he must find the strength to turn his head out of the dust that was strangling him. He fought to roll his head over on his cheek and succeeded in getting his mouth out of the dirt; then in the dimness he saw a man approaching stealthily from the corner of the barn. The man was waving his arms at the milling horses, moving slowly toward Will, as if he could not quite see him. This man, Will knew in cold dread, would be the man who would finish him off as soon as the milling horses were out of the way.

With all the ebbing strength he could summon, Will moved his right arm stretched out over his head, crooking the elbow, bringing the gun into the oncoming man's path. Sighting was impossible, for at the moment he could not lift his head. It would be a poor shot and likely his last, he knew, but there would be a shot if he could marshal the strength to pull back the hammer. With a savage effort of will he managed it, and then guessing where the gun was pointing, hoping wildly, he pulled the trigger.

Almost with indifference, pain overwhelming him,

he heard the man grunt and then felt the faint tremor of the earth as the man fell.

What followed was silence, except for the diminishing sound of the horses milling; no gunfire roused the night, no voice spoke, and the minutes raveled out, timed only by the rise and fall of his tortured breathing. *What are they waiting for?* he thought bleakly.

When still nothing happened, his terror started to ebb, letting reason into a small part of his mind. He had downed one of the men sent to kill him. The two stockdrivers, probably knowing nothing of the planned ambush, had fled away from trouble. That left the man with the shotgun who might be waiting, afraid to come out. Or perhaps Will's shot had either killed or wounded him. He might even be on his way for reinforcements this very moment.

Lying there, feeling the pain a steady torment, Will knew that he must get out of here or die, and it must be now. His first effort to rise brought a shattering wave of pain to his side and back and left shoulder. As he achieved his knees, sweat drenched his body and he no longer cared if the man with the shotgun was waiting. Now, with his right hand, he lifted his left hand and tucked it into his belt, easing the pain a little. On his knees then, he lurched the ten feet to the barn and there managed to claw himself erect, feeling the warm blood pool in the small of his back. He knew with a desperate awareness that he must stop this bleeding at all costs. But before he could do that, he must get out of here.

He lurched toward the door of the vet's cupboard, reached it, and felt his way through it and into the feed barn. If he stopped here, he knew he would be trapped, and he kept stubbornly on toward the far door. Achieving it, he stepped out into the night. Already he heard quiet voices back of the corral. Knowing they would probably track him by the blood he was trailing, he locked the door, hoping to gain an extra minute. Then, staggering out into the night behind the blacksmith shop, he made for the deep darkness behind Maydet's store a hundred yards away. Once there he halted, looking back at the corral where a lantern was already lighted. He had time now to tend himself.

Steeling himself against the torture that was sure to come, he clawed out of his coat, then pulled it off over his left shoulder and arm. He could feel pieces of the cloth that had been driven into his flesh tear away from his back and side as he pulled off his coat. Once the coat was free, he let himself down to a kneeling position and in the darkness rolled the tail of the holed coat up toward the collar. With the sleeves extended, it made a wide belt, and now he worked the coat across his left shoulder and back and under his right arm, holding a sleeve in his teeth to anchor it. Then, in fumbling and painful haste, he tied the two sleeves together across his chest, drawing them tight enough to press his left arm against the raw wound in his side. The coat too pushed the shredded flesh of his back against his body. Finished, he leaned against the logs of the store, waiting for the fresh pain to subside a little, closing his eyes against the drench of perspiration that was his body's protest against the pain.

When he opened his eyes, he saw several horsemen gathered around the lantern by the feed barn and he knew they were making their plans to hunt

him down. Knowing he was hurt, Maydet would
have them search every building until they found
him and killed him. There was no time to find Dickert and ask him for shelter. They would kill young
Bert too. In that moment the bleak realization of his
predicament came to him. He was badly hurt, losing
strength and on the run. To rest would be to die. His
only safety lay in movement, and he felt too weak to
move.

Pushing himself away from the building, Will
knew what he must do and do quickly. He turned
and staggered along the rear of Maydet's store and
past the back of the saloon, his body half bent
against the pain. Rounding the corner, he moved
toward the street and came up to the plankwalk between the log shack next to the saloon. There were
perhaps a dozen ponies still at the tie-rail, their own-
ers sticking with the late games inside.

Will knew he had only minutes of grace. When
the corrals, stables, and shops were searched as the
most likely places for him to be hiding, the search
would spread to the other buildings in town.

Forcing his back straight despite the pain, Will
stepped out onto the walk, crossed it, and moved
through the break in the tie-rail to nearest horse.
The smell of blood upon him made the pony snort
and move uneasily back until the tied reins were
taut. Will spent a desperate ten seconds trying to
soothe the horse, then gave it up, and moved on to
the next pony, who seemed more calm. He untied its
reins and moved up to the stirrup. Mounting, he
knew bleakly, would use up the last of his strength.
His foot in the stirrup, Will gathered all his strength;
with his right hand he grasped the horn; then sum-

moning his willpower, he pulled and pushed and fought until he lay belly down across the saddle. The horse was only a little restless under him, and he waited a minute until his strength came back. Then he inched his leg over the horse's rump and finally pulled himself into the saddle.

Down the road he could hear men calling to each other. He reined his horse around, heading into the blessed darkness of the prairie to the west.

Maydet's men would beat the town tonight, he knew, and come daylight they would search every building in it. Once they were certain he was not in the town, the search would spread to every station and every building on this division and in the next two. Maydet, knowing he was hurt, would be relentless, implacable, and swift. Dismally, Will knew that he had his choice of dying here on the prairie or finding someone who could hide him. That someone would risk death too.

Blindly then he rode west, not knowing where he was going and too full of pain to care. Instinct told him he must put as many miles as possible between Louisburg and himself while he could still ride. Later, when he began to shiver until he could barely hold himself in the saddle, the real nightmare of pain began. He would ease out of unconsciousness, not knowing how long his mind had been blanked. Each time he would look at the stars to make sure he was still traveling west, but later he found that his sight was so dim he could not even see the stars. Once he thought he heard a dog barking in the distance, but he only accepted this as part of the nightmare.

Sometime in the night, when he was either asleep

or unconscious, he slacked out of the saddle and fell heavily onto the prairie. The shock of the pain roused him, but there was nothing he could do before he slipped back into unconsciousness. After that his horse started to graze away from him.

He was first conscious of the pain caused by a steady jolting, and when he opened his eyes he was looking at grey canvas above him. He was so savagely thirsty that he could not even wonder where he was, and he was too weary to stifle the long shuddering groan of pain. The jolting suddenly ceased, and when he next opened his eyes he was looking into a bearded face between him and the canvas.

"Water," he whispered.

The face disappeared and he heard voices. His eyes closed again before he felt the water on his face. Then it cascaded into his mouth and he drank greedily, swallowing until his throat ached and he had to turn his face aside. Opening his eyes once more, he saw the face above him.

"Turn me over," he whispered.

Gently he was rolled over onto his belly and some of the pain slacked off.

"Can you hear me?" the voice asked.

"Yes."

"We found you on the prairie this morning and reckoned you wouldn't live."

"Come closer," Will whispered.

His eyes shut; he could hear breathing close to his ear. "You going west?" Will asked.

"We're headed for Oregon."

Will was so desperately tired that he could not

frame the words in his mind. Finally he said, "Have you passed a stage station?"

"A sod shack with an Indian woman there?"

"White house, new barn going up," Will whispered.

"No."

Will summoned all his strength to get the words out. "Put me down there."

The breathing came closer to his ear and then receded. "I think he's gone," the voice said, as Will slipped off into unconsciousness again.

The racket of the pounding on the porch door reached Carrie's small room off the kitchen, waking her and filling her with a faint apprehension. She heard Lennor moving upstairs and then heard him descend and cross the common room.

"Who's there?" he shouted, before unbolting the door.

Carrie did not hear the answer, but almost immediately heard the bolt slip and then the distant sound of voices. Presently she saw faint lamplight and then it became brighter as Lennor came into the kitchen and put down the lamp. Carrie next saw Lennor framed in the doorway of her room, trousers pulled on over his nightshirt. "You'd better get up, Carrie, I'll need help."

"What is it?"

"Gannon. He's shot bad. We'll take him into the bunkhouse. You'd better heat up some water and bring some rags and salve. Bring that bottle of whiskey, too."

Lennor turned away and Carrie hurriedly began to dress in the dark. A kind of nameless fear touched her. Shot bad, Mr. Lennor had said. She had predicted it and known that it would come, but now that it was here she felt nothing but fear.

Entering the kitchen, she hurriedly stirred up the fire, put more water on, rounded up the whiskey and bear grease and rags, lifted the tea kettle, and went out the back door, picking up the basin from a bench on her way.

The lamp was burning in the bunkhouse and Carrie remembered that sleeping inside were two men who had laid over from the eastbound stage. In this emergency she knew they wouldn't mind if a woman invaded their quarters. At the door, however, she halted and called, "Can you help me, Mr. Lennor?"

Lennor came to the door and relieved her of the basin and kettle, then turned back, and Carrie followed him in. The two passengers were in their bunks propped up on their elbows, watching. A strange man stood between Carrie and Gannon. When he moved aside to make way for Lennor, Carrie caught sight of Gannon lying on his face in the bunk, stripped to his waist; for a moment she thought she was going to faint. His upper back and side and part of his upper arm were raw and bloody meat.

Carrie turned to the table, trying to keep her hands from trembling as she poured water into the basin. It did not seem possible to her as she moved across to him with the basin that he could live with this great wound. His trousers were stiff to the boots with dried blood and as she looked at the wound she could see shreds of cloth that had been driven into it by the buckshot.

She looked inquiringly at Lennor and he shrugged

helplessly. "He's unconscious. I think we'd better clean him up before we give him whiskey."

Carrie nodded and set about her gruesome task. When the wound was washed, Lennor took out his knife and, his face as stern as Carrie had ever seen it, he set about probing out the visible buckshot that was embedded in Gannon's flesh.

There was nothing left to do now but smear bear grease over Gannon's back and cover the wound with cloth. When she was finished Carrie looked down at Gannon's drawn face, drained of all color, and she found herself looking for death in those tough features. Straightening up, she looked at the stranger and said, "Where did you find him?"

"This—yesterday morning it was, on the prairie. No horse, nothing. He had his coat tied across his arm and back. We loaded him in our wagon, sure that he would die. He came awake long enough to tell us to put him down at a white house where a new barn was going up. We traveled all night to reach here."

"Thank you for that," Carrie said and shuttled her glance to Lennor. "Wouldn't some whiskey and hot water bring some life into him?" Carrie asked.

"Try it. Try something," Lennor said glumly.

Carrie moved over and picked up Keefe's cup from beside the bunk where he was sleeping, then mixed warm water and whiskey in it. Kneeling beside Gannon, she raised his head and forced the cup between his lips, letting the water and whiskey trickle between his lips. At first he would not swallow and then she saw the muscles of his neck move as he took his first sip.

His eyes opened briefly and then closed, and Carrie took the cup away. His lips moved in an effort to speak and Carrie put her head closer. Gannon whispered briefly and now Carrie looked up at Lennor.

"What did he say?" Lennor asked.

" 'Hide me. They'll come.' "

Gently, still watching Lennor, Carrie laid Gannon's head back on the pallet and came erect.

"Hide him?" Lennor demanded desperately. "How do we hide him?" He looked helplessly at the immigrant who had brought Gannon but the man only shook his head. "We can't take him out on the prairie. He can't travel."

"Under my bed, Mr. Lennor," Carrie said quietly. "If anyone comes I'll be in bed, sick. No one would bother a sick woman, would they?"

"I'm a peaceful man," Lennor said grimly. "What would they do to us if they found him?"

"I'll take the blame," Carrie said. "If they find him, you can be surprised."

"If they find him, they'll kill him," Lennor said quietly. "They might kill you, too."

"I know," Carrie said quickly and, lest Lennor change his mind, she said to the immigrant, "Will you help us carry him once more?"

The bearded man nodded, saying, "I'll get my brother." He left the bunkhouse and returned in a moment with a younger man. With the two brothers at the head of Gannon's straw-filled pallet and with Lennor and Carrie at the foot, they lifted him and carried him in the darkness to the house where they laid him on the kitchen floor. Then Carrie and Lennor moved her bed, whose head had been against the kitchen wall, into the middle of the narrow room and the four of them laid Gannon on the floor where the bed had been. Gently they lifted the bed over him. Standing in the doorway, Carrie regarded her room as if she were a stranger looking in. Her bed to her left was larger than the narrow bunk pallet and more than covered it; unless a person got down on his knees and looked under the bed, he could not see Gannon.

Carrie said to the men then, "You'll want breakfast."

First, however, Carrie knew she must clean up all signs of Gannon's presence in the bunkhouse. Entering it, she took down a fresh pallet and blankets from an upper corner bunk and put them on Gannon's bunk while the two passengers watched her. Then, gathering up the basin, the kettle, the whiskey, and the salve, she paused and regarded the two stage passengers.

"You hold a man's life in your hands," she said. "They may be asking you about him."

"It's no business of mine, lady," one of the passengers said. "I didn't see anything."

"I've been asleep," the second passenger said.

Carrie smiled in thanks, looked in on Keefe, who was sleeping, then blew the lamp and returned to the house in the greying light of false dawn.

While Lennor and the two brothers talked around the kitchen table, Carrie busied herself with breakfast, thinking of Gannon. She wondered dismally what had happened and where the ambush took place, for she was sure it had been an ambush. Gannon, she knew, was not a man who would turn his back and run, and he had been shot in the back. But the fact that he had been found afoot on the prairie puzzled her. She knew her curiosity must wait on the arrival of the westbound stage driver who would have news of all that had happened between here and Louisburg.

At breakfast the two stocktenders joined them in the kitchen. They were sleeping outside now, but Lennor was taking no chances that they might have observed Gannon being unloaded from the immigrant wagon. He warned them sternly that they were to forget any activity they had witnessed last night on peril of losing their jobs.

Once breakfast was finished and full daylight was come, the bearded man and his brother thanked Lennor and left the house for their ox team. Carrie and Lennor trailed them out.

The bearded man touched his hat to her and Carrie said, "You can do us a last favor if you will."

"What's that, ma'am?"

"You'll be passing other stations and the news of this shooting will have traveled ahead of you."

The bearded man nodded, understanding. "We travel all day and camp at night, so we don't know anything about what's been happening."

"That's it," Carrie said. "Bless you both."

When their ox-drawn wagon was in motion, headed west, Carrie felt a faint relief. At least all visible signs of the way Gannon could have been transported here were gone. Lennor was already headed for the house, doubtless to acquaint Mrs. Lennor with everything that had happened. Carrie looked out over the prairie to the east. It was empty and she could not even see the distant speck of a traveler, but she knew trouble was coming. All she could do was wait.

She found the Lennors in the kitchen, and by the

frightened expression on Mrs. Lennor's face she knew that Lennor had told her what was planned.

"I've asked Mother to keep watch from the porch, Carrie. When she sees anyone coming, she'll warn you. I'll be working on the barn and they'll likely stop with me first. That will give you time to get off your clothes and get in bed."

"I don't like this," Mrs. Lennor said grimly. "We're paid to run a station, not to hide gunfighters."

"He's your employer," Carrie pointed out.

"That makes no difference," Mrs. Lennor said stubbornly. "This shouldn't be asked of us."

"You'd let them kill him?"

"They'll kill him in the end," Mrs. Lennor said, almost angrily. "If they find him here, they'll punish us."

"I've thought about that," Lennor said. "The story is that I slept out with the boys last night. Nothing awakened you, Mother, and nobody was wakened in the bunkhouse. This is to be all Carrie's doing." He looked at Carrie. "What are you going to say if they find him?"

"I haven't thought, because they won't. If they should, I'll think of something."

"Think of it now, girl," Lennor said, almost angrily. "The least we have at stake is our home and our living. You can't ask us to risk that by telling them we helped hide him. Think of something now."

They were both watching her and anger touched Carrie for a brief moment. They were afraid and they were putting the responsibility for their fear upon her. She wondered bitterly what Lennor would have done with Gannon if she had not been here.

Like Pilate, would he have washed his hands and turned away? At that moment, under their angry challenging stares, Carrie felt lonely, wrathful, and almost reckless. If she was the only person who stood between Will Gannon and death, then well enough. She would stand, not beg on her knees.

"I'll tell them he's been my lover," Carrie said flatly. "I'll tell them he's come to me many a time at night when you two were asleep and knew nothing about it. I'll tell them that's what he did last night and that I hid him."

"Disgusting!" Mrs. Lennor said.

"Isn't it?" Carrie responded angrily. "It's disgusting that I have to make up a story to protect you."

"That's enough, Carrie!" Lennor said sharply.

"You asked me to think of it now and I've thought of it!" Carrie said hotly. She turned and went into her room and shut the door. As she sat on the bed, she found herself trembling with anger. In the years she had been with the Lennors this was the first time she had ever lost her temper or spoken her mind. Now the Lennors had a perfect right to ask her to leave. They even had a right to tell the men hunting Gannon just where he could be found. She should not have let her anger push her into saying the things she had said, she thought miserably. She should have been meek and submissive, guiding Lennor into doing the right thing by letting him believe he had thought of it himself. But their small meaching concern for their property when a man's life was at stake had pushed her into speaking rashly.

A moaning sound from Gannon interrupted her thoughts and she knelt down and peered under the bed. He lay on his belly, face toward the room, as they had left him, and Carrie watched him a moment to see if he stirred. He lay utterly still and Carrie wondered wildly if the moaning sound was the death rattle. When she finally caught the rhythm of his deep even breathing a sick relief flooded her. Rising, she knew she must be about her work immediately, lest she anger the Lennors even more. Entering the kitchen, she saw Mrs. Lennor cleaning up the breakfast litter and silently she joined her as if nothing had happened between them.

Shouldn't she be on the porch keeping watch? Carrie wondered. Mrs. Lennor, however, continued to clear the table, and when that was finished she brought out the bread pan and began to mix dough. Presently, when she could stand it no longer, Carrie said, "I'll do that, Mrs. Lennor. You can go watch."

"I'll do nothing of the kind," Mrs. Lennor said grimly. "I'll have nothing to do with this. Nothing."

She looked up at Carrie and the two women regarded each other with open hatred. Mrs. Lennor was refusing even the small but necessary help her warning would give. This, Carrie knew, was Mrs. Lennor's punishment for Carrie's loss of temper.

It was during the rush of work brought on by the feeding of the eastbound stage passengers that Carrie first noticed the sound. It was a steady moaning that she could not identify at first, and then she knew. She paused in her work long enough to open her bedroom door. The moaning was louder and with it were fragments of words, sometimes a whole sentence. With mounting dread, Carrie knew that Gannon's wound had pushed him into delirium. A delirious person, she knew, sometimes fought savagely and shouted things never remembered afterwards. Unless Will's delirium subsided, how was she going to control either his actions or the noise he made?

Closing the door, she went about her work with an agonizing sense of helplessness. Either Mrs. Lennor was deaf or was skillfully pretending that the noises coming through the door from Carrie's room simply did not exist.

The conversation of the passengers and the clatter of the serving smothered the noises now, but what about the time when the house was empty save for the men hunting Gannon?

After the stage pulled out, carrying with it the two passengers who had seen Will, Carrie felt a measure of relief. Gannon's moaning subsided a little, but only a little, as Carrie washed the dishes at the stove. From there she could look through the common room out the porch door to where Lennor and his helpers were raising the barn. Almost finished with the dishes, she glanced out to Lennor and this time saw him talking to a rider whom she instantly identified by his massive figure in the saddle, as Lou Maydet, former division agent.

Terror touched Carrie. Here they were at last and now it was up to her to fight them alone. Through the door she could hear Gannon's quiet, incoherent talk. Quickly then she pushed the dishpan to the back of the stove and slipped into her room.

Taking off her dress, she pulled her full-sleeved nightgown on over her shift and then took off her shoes. Quickly tying a scarf around her neck, she opened the door and looked through the common room to the barn. No one was there. Now she moved to the kitchen window and saw three men, followed by Lennor, heading for the bunkhouse. Maydet, like an old buffalo bull, led the way. Behind him was Richie Cleff, whose lazy, catlike walk held a threat that Carrie could not define. Following Cleff was one of the notorious Louisburg roughs, a half-breed named Jim Cardman. Obviously Lennor had offered to show them the bunkhouse, where they would find only Keefe. Most certainly they would ask next to search the house. Behind her, through the closed door, Carrie heard Gannon's rambling moaning conversation in his fevered nightmare. With rising terror, Carrie knew she had only a minute to quiet him.

Running back into the room, she looked about her, then spied the heavy crockery water pitcher which stood in its basin on the washstand. Swiftly she emptied the remaining water into the bowl, and regarded the bed. It was too heavy for her to move alone, she knew, and besides there was not the time. Kneeling by the bed, she looked under it and saw Gannon lying on his back, arms at his side, his head rolling slowly in delirium as he moaned. Steeling herself, Carrie seized the pitcher by the handle and then with a sweeping stiff-arm movement she swung it at his head. It caught him on the point of the jaw with a sickening violence. Carrie waited the few seconds it took her to make sure that her blow had struck him unconscious. Then she rose, replaced the pitcher, and plucked a handkerchief from the drawer of her mean dresser. Loosening her hair, she wadded the handkerchief and stuffed it into her cheek. The handkerchief pouched out half her features, giving her the look of a person with all the signs of having a wildly abscessed jaw.

Slipping under the covers now, she lay on her back listening. It was only seconds before she heard the heavy tramp of boots on the back porch. They approached her door and halted and she heard Lennor say, ". . . been sick for three days. If you want, take a look." Carrie moaned softly and then heard the door open. Turning her head so that her swollen cheek was visible, she looked up slowly as would a fevered person trying painfully to focus upon an object in the doorway. Hulking massively above her stood Lou Maydet, his dark face watchful and alert. A gun trailed from the arm hanging at his side.

He glanced swiftly about the room, then turned and spoke to someone behind him. "You tried whiskey?"

"All we had. It helped some." This was Lennor's voice.

Heavily, Maydet turned in the doorway and Carrie groaned almost inaudibly. Her heart pounding, she heard Maydet say, "What's upstairs?"

Then she heard the sound of footsteps diminishing as the men tramped into the common room and mounted the stairs.

Carrie lay there listening, her heart almost bursting in her breast. Under her she felt rather than heard Gannon stir and silently she prayed, *Let them get out now, now!* Above stairs she heard a brief rumble of conversation and then the stairs creaked as the four men descended. She listened with desperate attention as they crossed the common room. Were they returning or were they leaving? When she heard the first footfall boom hollowly on the veranda, she expelled her breath in a long sigh. Swiftly then she rose, closed the door, and leaned against it, unable to stop shaking.

The first thing Will was conscious of was that it was night. The second was the scent of a woman's hair that seemed to come from the bedding in which his face was buried. The third thing he became aware of was that his body was as drenched with wetness as if he had just been pulled from water.

Turning his head, he studied the small square of window through which he could see stars and through which he could hear the soft rustle of wind on grass.

He had no notion of where he was, and when he tried to push himself to his elbows and look about the room the knifing pain slashed across his back and he subsided. Slowly, painstakingly, he tried to piece memory together. He remembered the ambush in the corral and his escape to the prairie. But how had he arrived here?

A faint rhythmic sound crept into his consciousness and for a long minute he listened, trying to locate the source and define it. Suddenly it came to him that the sound was that of someone breathing in this same room. He thought about this for a moment, considering what it meant. It could not mean that he was a prisoner, since Maydet would never have bothered to take him alive. That meant the person in the room was a friend.

When he was sure of his reasoning, he cleared his throat and said, "Where am I?" He heard the breathing cease and repeated his question.

He heard someone stirring in the room and then

the flare of a match blinded him and made him turn his head away. When the light steadied into a glow he knew must be lamplight, he turned his face away from the wall and saw Carrie Bentall standing by the lamp on the dresser. Her pale hair was loosely braided in a pigtail and she was tying the belt of a worn wrapper as she moved to his side. Will took the dipper of water she was holding out to him and drank greedily. Handing it back, he looked up at her and saw how drawn her features were and how tired she looked.

"When did I get here, Carrie?" he asked.

"Six days ago," Carrie said.

"How?"

"An emigrant found you on the prairie."

"Maydet didn't come for me?" Will asked.

Carrie nodded. "He's long come and gone. We hid you."

Will considered this, almost too tired to give it the thought it deserved.

Yet in spite of his weakness, he was singularly clearheaded in the wake of his fever. Carrie moved out of the room into the kitchen carrying the lamp, and now Will thought of what she had said. Where had she hidden him that Maydet couldn't find him?

He dozed a little and was awakened again by the lamp. Carrie set it on the floor, then, kneeling by the bed, she said, "Can you eat this?"

Will caught the smell of meat broth and hunger came so swiftly that it was almost pain. Lying on his belly, holding the bowl in his hand, he drank it down. Twice Carrie took it and refilled it before Will had enough.

Returning from the kitchen, Carrie knelt to pick

up the lamp. Will said, "Stay there a minute, Carrie."

She sat back on her heels and with that gesture that had become so familiar to Will she brushed her pale hair off her forehead with the back of her wrist. She looked exhausted, Will thought, but oddly there was an expression of contentment, even happiness, in her dark eyes. It was as if she had achieved a victory while enough strength remained to appreciate it.

"Hid me where?" Will asked.

Quietly Carrie told him of hiding him under the bed, of hushing his delirious ramblings by smashing him on the jaw with the pitcher. Her ruse of pretending an infected tooth had taken Maydet in and he had not disturbed the room. When Will reflected on this and on the courage and daring it had taken to pull it off, he felt guilty, humble, and sad rather than grateful. Nothing he had ever said to this girl or done for her deserved this kind of devotion. On the contrary, his roughness should have earned her indifference. How had she cared for his wound, he wondered, since he remembered once being sure that he would die.

"What's my back like, Carrie?"

"The fever and the poison are out of it," Carrie said. "That happened yesterday."

Mention of the fever reminded Will that of the past six days he could remember nothing. Carrie had had to hit him to quiet his delirious ravings, she had said.

Watching her carefully now, Will asked, "When I was off my head, did I talk, Carrie?"

She only nodded.

"About what?"

Carrie waited a long moment, as if hesitant about answering. "About Marian." She paused. "She must have meant a lot to you, Will."

Will thought of this, and oddly, the memory was not even disturbing now. He said quietly, "She was my wife, Carrie. She ran away with another man and then took her own life."

"I know," Carrie said. "I've had six days and nights to piece that together."

Weariness overcame him and he laid his head on the blanket, but his eyes were open, watching her. She made to rise, but with his open palm he gestured her to stay and she sank back on her heels.

"I thought nothing good would ever happen to me after that, but I was wrong, Carrie."

A faint smile lifted the corner of Carrie's mouth. "You call this good?"

Will's eyes closed with weariness. "I do," he said.

There were other questions he must ask her. Tiredly he tried to think of them and presently he asked, "Is the division all right?"

"There's been no trouble that we've heard of."

Will felt a stir of relief at her answer. The past six days would have been the time for Maydet to strike if he wanted, since there was neither a division agent nor a division superintendent on the job. But he had a feeling there was something else, something important, that he had left undone before the ambush, and he tried to flag his weary brain into remembering. Finally it came to him that it was the specie shipment and he asked, "Has a messenger coach come through?"

"One eastbound," Carrie said.

Then the specie shipment had not gone through heading west. Will remembered now that he had planned to send to Salt Lake for reliable guards, but it was too late now. Young Bert Dickert would have to do the best he could with the men he had in Louisburg. His best, Will thought wearily, had to be good enough.

Minutes passed, and when Carrie saw that he slept, she blew the lamp and went back to her straw pallet at the foot of Will's bed.

Wilsey Kirk, at the corner of Bates Boley's barn, drank sparingly from the tin cup of whiskey before him and observed to himself for perhaps the fiftieth time that Boley's whiskey was as bad as his daughter's cooking. Apparently, his band of midnight passengers preferred the whiskey, for they thronged the bar and left their food untouched. Wilsey took his last sip, shuddered, straightened, said, "When you're ready, gentlemen," and moved out into the room, drawing on his gauntlets.

A movement in the kitchen door attracted Wilsey's attention and he glanced over to see Hutch Forney enter the room. He was whistling thinly and when he saw Wilsey a quick grin came to his handsome, reckless face.

Approaching Wilsey, he said, "I thought you had a lay-over."

"Bailey was sick," Wilsey said sourly. "Likely from eating here." Shrewdness crept into his eyes. "You seem to like the food here, though."

Hutch only grinned. "It's the whiskey," he said. "I never thought I'd have to climb a mountain for it, but I do. Got room for me?"

"On top," Wilsey said.

Hutch stood beside him watching the passengers file out and presently he asked, "Any word on Gannon?"

Wilsey snorted. "He's dead."

"He don't kill easy," Hutch said quietly.

Wilsey looked at him. "Hell, there was a tub of blood not fifteen feet from where they found Harry Coons."

"All right, he got Bill Ferry afterwards, didn't he? He got up and walked away, didn't he?"

"Then where is he?" When Hutch did not answer, Wilsey said, "I figure he crawled out on the prairie to die."

Hutch didn't want to answer, for he was afraid that Wilsey was right.

When the passengers were loaded, Hutch climbed up into the seat behind the box. He discouraged all attempts at conversation by Wilsey and the express messenger, and presently they left him alone. Hutch wanted to think, for with Gannon gone things were changed. Even if Gannon was alive and returned, Hutch knew that he had lost his chance of becoming division agent by his first clandestine visit to Boley's. He hated the loneliness of the Dry Creek Station where Gannon had kept him as punishment. Maggie, however, had been worth that. Now that he had her, he wondered what he was going to do.

The first thing, the overriding thing, was to kill Maydet. In open fight or ambush, it didn't matter. Tough Will Gannon might not be Midland's division superintendent any more, but Maydet would never live to succeed him. But after he killed Maydet, then what?

There was his brown, pregnant wife and the coffee-colored child at Helper Creek. Was he really married to this alien woman? Did a heathen ceremony really constitute a marriage between a white man and an Indian? It wasn't his religion that bound them; it wasn't even the laws of his country. Then what did? Why couldn't he take Maggie and just leave the country? His wife had a house and some horses. With forty dollars a month the line paid her, she could eat and still pay a stocktender. Pretty soon the kids could take over and help. All in all, he had provided for them better than their own people ever could have. Meanwhile he could have a woman of his own kind married to him legally and in a white man's religion. With a new start somewhere else, no one need ever know about the Indian woman and the two kids.

They changed teams at Soderstrom's and after that Hutch slept, holding to the iron rail of his seat. Before they approached the last of the foothills and Dry Creek Station in the dawn, Hutch wakened and knew he had come to his decision. He would stick here and wait to see if Gannon showed up. If he didn't, there was Maydet to take care of. That would mean he would have to leave the country, and in leaving the country he would take Maggie with him.

A half-mile from the station Hutch noticed an unfamiliar object out on the prairie to the south and at the same time Wilsey asked, "What've you got out there?" As they came closer Hutch stood up on the seat for a better view, and when he was sure he said softly, "Wilsey, it looks like a coach on its side."

Wilsey whipped the tired teams into a gallop, and as the stage approached closer they confirmed

Hutch's observation. It was a stage tipped on its
side, a horse lying beneath it. Then the three of
them were looking at the hard-packed yard around
the station. It was only when the lead team veered
off the road, as if reluctant to approach, that Wilsey
spoke. "I count four men."

Forty yards from the station Wilsey reined up and
kicked on the brake. Hutch hit the ground a little
before Wilsey and the messenger, and he was running. When he came to the first body, stretched
belly-down, he halted and Wilsey pulled up beside
him. Hutch's glance shuttled to the second body
forty feet away. The sightless eyes of Tim Mayze, a
driver they both knew, were open to the sun. Closer
to the house was a third boy, the chest torn open,
and beside it lay the fourth, face-down.

Now Hutch glanced over at the stage where a single dead wheel horse was pinned to the earth under
a shattered tongue and wheel festooned with broken
harness.

Wilsey said quietly, "Specie shipment with three
guards. They must have waited inside and blown
them off the coach when they stopped. The teams
stampeded and kicked free, but they'll have got the
gold."

An overwhelming knowledge that this was true
and that it would have never happened if he had
been here came to Hutch. Then he buried his face in
both hands, unable to look, his own guilt unbear-
able.

6

Will came awake as soon as the door opened, raising his head which had been pillowed on the forearm of the hand that held his gun. It was Carrie. She stepped into the room and closed the door, shutting out the clatter of the passengers in the common room.

Will saw the still alarm in her face and he asked, "Somebody here?"

Carrie shook her head slightly. "Can you see Wilsey?"

"I can see anyone now, even Maydet. What is it, Carrie?"

Carrie didn't answer, but went out of the room. Will pushed himself off his belly to a kneeling position, then swung his feet to the floor. He was sitting on the edge of the bed when the door opened and Wilsey Kirk stepped into the room.

Wilsey hauled up and his bearded jaw slacked open and there was instantaneous shock in his pale eyes. "Well, by God," Wilsey breathed.

Carrie moved in behind him and closed the door and now Wilsey said, with grim humor, "I had you dead. I had the coyotes cracking your bones, Gannon."

"Just so Maydet thinks that, too, Wilsey."

Will's inquiring glance shuttled to Carrie, who said, "Tell him, Wilsey."

Wilsey said, matter-of-factly, "The specie coach was held up at Dry Fork. I don't reckon you'd call it a hold-up exactly, because the driver and three guards were killed. Murdered. From all the signs three men forted up in the 'dobe. When the coach pulled in for the team change the three guards and the driver were just blowed off the coach. It looks like the teams went wild then. They kicked hell out of the coach, turned it over, killed a wheeler, and kicked free of the traces. The boot was empty."

As Will listened to Wilsey's words, he felt his heart go out of him, and for a terrible moment he wanted to put his hands to his ears to shut out Wilsey's story. These were his men, murdered, the men he was pledged to protect. It took him stunned seconds to accept the enormity of this cynical massacre and then, when his mind finally began to work, he asked the one question that Wilsey seemed to be expecting.

"Wilsey, where was Hutch?"

"At Boley's."

Will looked at him a long, long moment, and then asked, "You know that yourself?"

"I brought him down. We come on it together."

A grey despair touched Will then and he looked down at the floor. *No! Hutch, no!* he thought wildly. In the seconds it took him to understand this, he could find no anger within him, only an overwhelming sadness. Hutch, loyal, courageous, and weak, was the true betrayer. If Hutch had been at Dry Fork, he would probably be dead now. Yet that

would have been better than living with the knowledge now locked in his mind.

Will lifted his grey face and his glance sought Carrie. She was watching him with a pity that Will could
not face. His glance shuttled to Wilsey and he asked,
"Who was the driver, Wilsey?"

"Tim Mayze."

"Was a gun fired from the stage?"

"All the guns were loaded but not fired," Wilsey
said grimly. "That's why I figure it was three men. If
it was any less, one of the guards would have got a
shot off. If it was any more, at least one of our men
would have been shot twice."

Will looked away, but Wilsey went on relentlessly,
"It looked like one guard was standing on top and
got wiped off. He was on his back. The second and
third guards were face-down. They was fairly close
together. Tim was farther off, face-down, like he'd
been drug a little before the reins was pulled out of
his hands."

"All right, Wilsey," Will said, in protest. "All
right."

Wilsey stood there uncertainly, but Will sat as if in
a stupor. Presently Wilsey said, "You want me to do
anything, Gannon?"

Will looked up at him, his eyes coming into focus,
then he took a deep, sighing breath. "Have Dickert
report to Olderson. Tell Dickert I'm alive, but no
one else, Wilsey. No one."

The driver nodded and moved past Carrie to the
door. As Wilsey put his hand on the knob, Will said,
"Just give me time, Wilsey."

"Sure," Wilsey said. His one word seemed to hold
understanding, patience, and a total withholding of

judgment. He stepped out and closed the door behind him.

Will looked at the gun that he had never put down and slowly laid it on the blanket. "Fix me up to travel, Carrie."

"You're not leaving!" Carrie said sharply.

Will shook his head. "You don't understand, Carrie. I can't do anything else."

"You can barely walk! You haven't any strength!" Carrie protested.

"You still don't understand," Will said softly. "Maydet thinks I'm dead, or too hurt to move. He knows there's no one but Dickert to run him down and Bert's only a boy. Can't you see now's the time I have to move?"

"But you can't!"

"Fix me up, Carrie," Will said, his voice patient but implacable.

Resignedly, Carrie went out and returned almost immediately with a bundle of clean rags and a jar of bear grease. She carefully removed Will's shirt and afterward the soiled bandage on his back. Then she spread the grease thinly over the clean linen and gently applied it to the raking wound across his back and under his arm. She put several layers of cloth over this and then tore off strips from a chunk of canvas. She anchored another grease-soaked pad in his armpit so that it rested against the torn flesh of his inner upper arm and, using the canvas strips, bound his arm against his side, moving the canvas strip around his back and across his chest.

When she was finished and had slipped on his shirt, Will stood up and tucked his left hand under his belt. His left arm was useless, but he would have to learn to accept that for some days to come. He knew from the practice walks he had taken around the common room for the last couple of days that he had strength enough to mount his horse, which was all that was required.

Now he said, "When Wilsey pulls out, have one of the boys bring my horse around to the back door."

Obediently Carrie moved toward the door, then turned. "Won't you take someone with you?"

"Hutch," Will said. "Tell Lennor to send one of his stocktenders to Dry Creek on the westbound."

"Is Hutch enough?"

"He's got four dead men riding with him. That's enough."

"And how many have you riding with you?" Carrie asked bitterly.

With surprise Will saw that she was angry. "What do you want me to do, Carrie?"

"You asked me that before and I told you. I don't know. Keep on riding through to California, maybe."

"And leave the government to recover its gold shipment? Leave four murders unpunished? Leave the line and every man who works on it in daily fear of his life?"

"You can't stop it!" Carrie said swiftly. "You've proven that!"

"Maybe I can't stop it, but I don't run from it," Will said grimly.

"That's right," Carrie said quickly. "You run *at* it. You'll run at it once too many times, Will. Maybe this is it."

"Maybe," Will conceded.

Carrie went out and in a few moments she returned with the information that Will's horse was outside the back door.

Slowly, on uncertain legs, Will went into the kitchen where Mrs. Lennor was cleaning up after the passengers' meal. She would not look at him, and Will knew that she hated his presence here and the risk it had brought on them. Outside, one of the stocktenders was holding a saddle horse, Carrie standing beside him. Will checked to make sure his rifle was in its scabbard. Alongside the coiled rope, his blanket roll was strapped behind his saddle and over the horn was his shell belt and holstered gun.

Walking up to his horse, he put his foot in the stirrup, grasped the horn with his right hand, and fought to raise himself into the saddle. He almost made it and then his legs refused to take his weight and he fell back. Looking at Carrie over the saddle, he saw that same look of pity that had angered him before. Savagely, he summoned all his strength and fought rather than climbed into the saddle. Once seated, he accepted the reins from the stocktender and looked at Carrie. "I don't know when I'll be back, Carrie."

"I do. Never."

"That could happen," Will said mildly. "If I don't come back though, it won't be because I'm in California."

"That didn't need saying."

Will reined his horse around and headed west over the prairie. It took him only a short time to discover that the motion of his horse did not bother his back, for Carrie's tight bandaging held his arm rigid to his side. With many days of riding ahead of

him, there was some small comfort in this knowledge.

Now his thoughts turned to speculation on what
the three stage robbers had planned by way of escape. They had more than a full day's head start.
But this time, Will knew, they would not fort up in a
mountain shack and wait for their pursuers. This
time they would have counted Gannon out, but in
counting him out they could count the U.S. marshal
in. It would take days to organize a search and during those days the three robbers would put as much
country as they could between themselves and the
Dry Creek Station. Logically, they would head for
the mountains and become lost in any of a hundred
remote and undiscovered canyons. They would not
expect immediate pursuit and in that, Will knew, lay
his advantage. If he pressed it, there was a slim
chance of overtaking them.

It was after dark when he reached Dry Creek Station. No light showed in the adobe, but as he approached, Hutch's iron challenge came from the
doorway. "Pull in right there!"

"It's me, Hutch. Gannon," Will called out.

He reined in and presently made out the dim figure of Hutch approaching him. "Speak again, Will,"
Hutch said warily.

"All right, help me off this horse."

Now Hutch came closer, his rifle ready. Then,
sure of his man, he came up. "You heard," Hutch
said. It was not a question but a statement.

"Yes. From Wilsey."

"Don't hack at me, Will," Hutch said quietly,
plain warning in his voice.

"I don't think I have to," Will said. "Hold these reins."

Hutch caught the reins and Will grasped the horn with his right hand, swung his leg over the saddle, and slid to the ground. For a moment, when his legs failed him, he held himself erect with his right arm, then slowly he let his legs accept his weight and he was only just standing.

"Give me my rifle," Will said.

When Hutch had taken the rifle from Will's scabbard and handed it to him, Will upended it and, using it as half cane, half crutch, he moved slowly toward the door.

"You all right?" Hutch asked.

Will grunted for answer.

He made the doorway and in the darkness moved wearily across the room to the straw pallet and sat on its edge.

He was seated thus when Hutch, after turning out his horse, came in with the lantern and set it on the table. The two men looked at each other in silence. Will saw, with quiet shock, that Hutch seemed to be moving as a man in a trance; his eyes, usually reckless and on the edge of humor, were sunken and dull. As he stirred up the fire, his movements were clumsy and without that spare quickness of movement that had once graced his every action.

When he had got the fire going, Hutch toed a round of firewood up to the table and sat down, looking across the table at Will.

"Who hid you, Will?"

"Carrie."

The hint of pleasure altered the bleak expression in Hutch's face for a moment, then vanished. He sighed, then said, "You can ask questions any time you're ready, Will."

Gannon said quietly, "Why were you at Boley's?"

Hutch said tonelessly, "Tom-cattin' with Maggie Boley."

Then that explained it, Will thought bleakly. Hutch had been after Maggie Boley and because of his lust four men were dead. There was no use saying any more to Hutch, he knew, and they would never talk of it again. Hutch's punishment would never cease and there was nothing he could add to it or subtract from it, he thought in a stupor of weariness.

When the stew began to bubble, Hutch rose and dished out Will's plate, handed it to him where he was sitting on the edge of the bed, and then went out. He returned with Will's blanket roll, spread it on the floor, then said, "You take the bunk."

Wearily Will handed him the half-finished plate of stew, saying, "This is once I won't argue. We start out at daylight." Pulling off his boots, he rolled over on his belly and eased himself down. His back throbbed dully and he knew he would have to wait for this to die down before sleep would come.

Hutch tidied the table, then blew the lamp, and Will could hear him pull off his boots and roll into his blankets.

Presently Hutch's voice came out of the darkness. "I buried four men today, Will. I wished each one of them was me."

"I know," Will said.

There was a long silence and Will hoped that Hutch was asleep, but Hutch's voice presently came again. "How do you live with something like this, Will?"

How many times had he himself wondered that after Marian's death? Wasn't he, in a way he did not understand, as guilty of her death as Hutch was of the death of four men? Somewhere along the way he had failed her, just as Hutch had failed his trust.

He answered then, "I don't know, Hutch. All I know is that you do."

Gannon did not even hear Hutch get up for the team change during the night and when he wakened at bare dawn Hutch had breakfast ready. The stocktender Lennor he had sent out on the westbound to hold down Dry Creek Station in Hutch's absence had already finished breakfast and when Will stood in the doorway to look at the morning, he saw him saddling up their horses.

Over a quick breakfast, Hutch told the little he had learned about the three men who had held up the specie coach. After the shootings, they had first confirmed that Tim Mayze and the three guards were all dead, then they had looted the coach. After presumably dividing the loot, one man had headed south while two cut back around the corral and headed north. The horses of these two men were shod and Hutch had trailed them long enough to memorize their tracks.

"We'll take the two," Will said. He saw the stirring of a feral pleasure in Hutch's eyes at his words. Gannon knew that all of Hutch's cunning and intelligence would be dedicated to this pursuit.

Breakfast finished, Will and Hutch went outside. Beyond the corrals Will saw the four freshly dug graves mounding the prairie, and alongside by the barns was the wrecked coach. Hutch looked at neither and when he accepted the reins of both horses from the stocktender and led them out, he avoided Will's eyes.

With less effort than it had taken yesterday, Will climbed into the saddle while Hutch watched covertly. Will had not talked of his wound and Hutch had not asked him about it, but Will knew that he was watching, gauging Will's ability to go through with this undertaking.

Riding out, Hutch soon picked up the tracks, and at the first bare spot the horse crossed he reined in and pointed out to Will how one of the horses, smaller than the other, toed in with his left foot so that the shoe cut deeper on its outside edge. Afterward they pushed on and by mid-morning were in the foothills. The sky held a faint overcast now and Hutch seemed to be studying it worriedly. At midday they came to the dry camp made by the killers at the edge of an empty creek bed. Here the two men had scooped out holes in the sand to obtain seep water for their mounts.

By afternoon, when they were in the timber of the mountains, the sky was fully overcast and a ground breeze moved steadily.

Was a rain coming? Will wondered.

The two horsemen ahead were traveling game trails now and Will began to see a pattern in their flight. They were heading roughly northwest, angling for the high country. When he was sure of it, Will waited until they paused at a meadow break in the timber and then he asked, "What are the mountains like to the north, Hutch?"

"They're some lower," Hutch answered. "I figure they're heading for a low pass. Anything above us would be drifted for another month."

Twice within the next hour Will reined up, and both times it was where the timber broke away at the edge of small grassy parks. Each time he rode slowly into the parks, studying the ground. The last time he dismounted painfully and moved about in a zigzag route, kneeling twice to examine the ground and the grass more thoroughly. At the far side of the second park he reined in and shook his head.

"It isn't sensible, but there it is."

"What?" Hutch asked.

"They've stopped to graze their horses—a good long time, too, if you can judge by the grass that's been grazed off."

"Today?"

Will looked at him and nodded, frowning. "I figure they made another dry camp in that first pasture. This one is pretty well grazed over. They loafed here most of the morning. I'd judge they're four or five hours ahead of us."

Will fell silent, trying to read meaning into the actions of the two men ahead of them. "I'll make my guess," he said presently. "They're not afraid of being followed. They're resting up their horses and grazing them, getting strength for the cross-over tomorrow."

"Then they won't be carrying grain," Hutch said.

"No. What's ahead, Hutch?"

"Let's find out before rain hits us," Hutch said. He reined his horse around and, picking up the tracks again, headed up the game trail that threaded the thick green timber. Wearily, Will mounted and followed. At a dead tree standing on the shoulder of the mountain, Hutch dismounted. It took him twenty minutes to climb to the very tiptop of the tall bare spruce and he remained there several minutes.

Once more on the ground, he came over to Will.

"We're heading into a wide canyon that climbs to a saddle. There may be peaks behind it, but I can't see them."

"Let's see if they head up the canyon," Will said.

It began to rain before dark. At first it was a misty drizzle with the far-off sound of thunder in the north. Within the hour, however, the sky opened up and they were in a wild driving thunderstorm, with lightning crackling down from the high peaks above. Before the driving rain had washed away the tracks, they had the confirmation they needed. The two horsemen ahead of them were traveling the game trails leading into the big canyon.

At full dark Hutch pulled off the trail under a sheltering spruce and waited for Will to rein in beside him. Both men were soaking wet and there was enough light for Hutch to see that Will's face was drawn and pale.

"If we're crossing over tomorrow, Will, you'd better get some rest. And so had the horses."

"Let's shoot the whole poke," Will said quietly.

Hutch frowned in puzzlement. "How do you mean?" he asked.

Wearily Will leaned forward to rest his right forearm on the horn. "If you were four hours up this canyon and ran into this rain and knew you were crossing over tomorrow, what would you do?" Will asked.

Hutch thought a moment. "I'd figure first of all

that my horses had to be fresh for the crossing. Then I'd figure this rain would be snow in a higher country and that up there I'd spend a hell of a night."

"So you'd switch over and camp on the south slope in thick timber and close to grazing, wouldn't you? You'd stake out your horses in the best grass you could find, dry out, feed up, and get the earliest start you could for the long day bucking snow on the cross-over. You'd want to give yourself time to turn back and make timber if the snow was too deep for your horses."

"That's right."

Will continued, "Then let's shoot the whole poke. Let's travel all night. We'll be on the north side of the canyon where the weather is, so there's little chance of us spooking them. Let's get as close to timberline as we can make it, then drop down to the stream at daylight. They'll hold to the stream grade because that's generally easiest. Besides, when they get to the snow the water will have cut the ice and snow."

Hutch considered this and then sighed. "We'll kill our horses and likely you, Will. How do you feel? Tell me the truth."

"If we keep going I'm all right," Will said grimly. "If I get off this horse, you'll be two days getting me back on. I'm in no shape for a long hunt, Hutch, and neither are our horses. Let's grain our horses and make the big gamble tonight. If we miss, then you can go on alone."

"I don't like it," Hutch said. "You're so beat you can barely talk. We could camp here, grain the horses, give you a rest, and start out early. We'd gain hours on them while they fought the snow. If they had to turn back, we'd have them cornered. If they crossed over, they'd likely spend a day in camp resting their horses. That's when we'd have them."

"That's when *you'd* have them, Hutch," Will said almost angrily. "I wouldn't be there at the finish, and I want to be."

"Then we travel," Hutch said.

Hutch grained the horses, and afterwards they ate Hutch's cold meat and biscuits. When they had finished, Hutch took off their blanket rolls and by cutting a hole in each of two blankets made a poncho apiece for them. It would not shed the rain but it would give them some warmth against the coming cold of the high country.

Will's back was aching almost like a live tooth; it seemed to him that he had never rested and never slept. He knew that by tomorrow he would be exhausted and at the end of his strength. He had told Hutch the bitter truth: as far as he was concerned, the next few hours must see the finish or he would have to give up.

There began then a night of purest hell. The rain kept to a dismal wind-driven drizzle from the north, a chilling, shocking misery that goaded them hour after hour. Hutch in the lead let his horse choose the way, only keeping him climbing ever higher, headed north and west. Time and again they came to steep feeder canyons which forced them higher through brush and timber that whipped their faces and at times almost tore them from the saddle. The country strange to them and their mounts, in the darkest kind of night and the worst conditions, they could only blunder on, but it was a stubborn, savage blundering that covered heartbreaking miles.

Sometime in the night Will felt fever return. A chill would shake him with a jaw-shattering violence and it would be followed by a wave of scalding fever that made him want to tear off his poncho and bare his body to the chill drizzle. During these times he could not remember why he was here. Later, when memory returned, the old stubbornness came with it. Once when they had thrashed endlessly in a slippery-floored aspen thicket whose trees seemed as close together as hair, Hutch had reined up and turned to Will. "We'll never make it, Will. We're crazy."

"Sure. Go on," Will said hoarsely. Afterwards, the timber started to thin out and Hutch quit climbing. The rain had turned to a snow which melted as it fell. Their horses now were staggering with weariness, but Will could be of little help to his mount. He could only concentrate on his wild determination to stay in the saddle.

Sometime about dawn they picked up the sound of rushing water to their right, and as daylight began to break they could make out the high shallow valley through which the stream ran. To their left and above were snow fields and Will saw through glazed eyes that they were close to the edge of timber. Great misty swirls of cloud and fog hid the peaks and the saddle. High to their right the last of the thick green timber bridged the stream where the canyon narrowed down, and Hutch, without even discussing it, pointed his horse toward it. Whoever wanted passage through these mountains at this spot must here take to the stream; the snowy precipitous slopes everywhere else bulked steep and impassable.

When they achieved the timber it was bare daylight, and their horses, walking with hung heads, were trembling under them with exhaustion. The stream, high here but not wide, presented only one more obstacle to the exhausted horses. They plunged into it with stumbling feet, bracing themselves against a fast but shallow current.

Once in the trees of the north bank, Hutch stepped wearily out of the saddle and moved over to where Will had reined in his horse. Will's cheeks were bright with fever, his eyes glittering, Hutch noticed.

"Find the spot, Hutch, before I move," Will said.

Stumbling with weariness, Hutch set off to the north through the close green timber. A hundred yards from their horses, he came to the edge of timber. Here a well-traveled game trail came down between big boulders to the stream. Beyond it, higher boulders choked off ready access to the stream before the canyon blended steeply into the mountain. If the two horsemen had camped on the north side of the stream in the thickest timber and held to that bank as they progressed, this would be the last place they could enter the stream course. Shaking with cold, Hutch moved up to the trail and saw the freshly made tracks of a buck which had come down to the stream earlier. The trail held no horse tracks and, turning, Hutch knew they were in time. Retracing his steps, he saw a tall dead pine on the edge of the timber and made a note that, once this business was over, here was firewood enough to warm them and dry them out.

When he returned to Will, he found him sleeping in the saddle, head slumped forward. Waking him, Hutch led Will's horse to the edge of the timber where he had an open view of the game trail less than thirty yards away. Will looked at it, nodded, and then tried to dismount. Leaning far forward in the saddle, he attempted to lift his right leg over, but it took Hutch's help to achieve it. Then he fell and Hutch caught him. The raw rub of Hutch's body against his back brought a shock of pain to him and he fought for enough strength in his legs to pull away from Hutch. Standing then, he saw the tree he wanted and staggered toward it. When he reached it, he sank to his knees and moved gently into a sitting position with his side against the tree.

Wordlessly Hutch turned Will's horse and led him back into the timber. The slow rain muffled all sound and Will did not even hear him go. Presently Hutch returned and knelt down beside him.

"What do you figure?" Hutch asked.

Will did not answer; he was asleep, chin on chest, hand slackly gripping his pistol. Hutch studied him, noting his gaunt face with the coming black beard stubble that seemed to blue its planes. Judging by his own bone weariness, he could only guess at the misery Will had suffered this night. His own eyes began to close and now, lest he fall asleep, he came wearily to his feet and leaned against the same tree.

Suddenly, as if born out of the misting rain, a doe appeared on the game trail. She halted, watching the stream below, and because Hutch was utterly still, her attention was not attracted. Satisfied that all was clear, she moved five feet down the trail when suddenly she froze, her head swiveling around toward the green timber, her glance passing Hutch until she was looking over her shoulder back up the trail. Her ears were erect and Hutch could see her nostrils quivering. Hutch strained to listen, too, and could hear nothing. But suddenly the doe leaped down the trail. In three springs she had reached the creek, jumped it, and vanished into the timber of the far bank.

Hutch knelt and put a hand on Will's shoulder, shaking him. It was Will's left shoulder and the pain of the contact roused him instantly, as he moved his shoulder aside.

"A deer just spooked past," Hutch whispered.

Will pushed his shoulder away from the tree. He knew he should be on his feet but at the moment he could not make it.

Kneeling beside him, Hutch whispered, "I'll take the first man. You take the second."

They waited, straining their ears to catch any new sound. Presently it came, the muffled chuck of a horseshoe on rock. Softly Will pulled back the hammer of his pistol. Again they heard, above the soft hush of the drizzling rain, the sound of metal hitting rock. In seconds they picked up the rhythmic clomping of a horse walking, and it was blended with the sound of a second horse.

Then all sound ceased and Will felt a faint alarm, wondering why they had halted. It came to him that they were probably halted at the edge of the bank, looking ahead up the creek to see what lay before them. Even as he was thinking this, he heard the horses move and now the sound was close. Then the head and shoulders of a horse appeared from behind the boulder, and the figure of a big man, part Indian, whom Will did not know, dressed in sodden clothes, came into sight; he was looking upstream. Following closely came the second horseman and Will felt a wild exultation at sight of him. It was Richie Cleff, and he was hunched slackly in the saddle as if in catlike shrinking from the rain.

"Cleff!" Will called. Both men swiveled their heads to look at the two men at the edge of the timber, their guns leveled.

The breed roweled his horse savagely, even as he turned his head and his horse lunged down the bank. Hutch's shot simply wiped the man out of the saddle, but Will did not see this; he was looking over his sights at Cleff. Cleff belatedly spurred his horse too, his hands lifting his rifle, butt first, from its scabbard. He pulled his horse to the left in a daring attempt to cut into the timber. And now Will, knowing he had lost Cleff in his sight, nevertheless pulled the trigger. The front legs of Cleff's horse folded under him and Cleff was catapulted headfirst out of the saddle against a tree. Will heard Cleff's muffled cry as he tried to raise his arm to cushion the blow and failed. He crashed into the tree headfirst, then fell on his knees and rolled on his side.

Hutch was already in motion, running for Cleff. Will pushed himself to his feet and lunged toward the trail where the half-breed lay face-down, his head toward the stream. Hutch, he knew, would take care of Cleff. Approaching the man, Will knelt and with his right hand rolled him over. The man's eyes were open, unseeing, and Will knew he was dead. Will rose and saw that Hutch had rolled Cleff over and was searching for his pistol under Cleff's pony coat.

Skirting the downed horse, Will noted that his shot had entered just ahead of the saddle skirt, killing the horse instantly.

Halting by Hutch, he looked down at Cleff. The flesh on Cleff's cheek was scraped raw from the bark on the tree and his eyes were closed. Hutch rose now and rammed Cleff's pistol in his belt. Then he turned and went back to Cleff's horse. Kneeling, he opened the saddle bag behind the saddle, and Will, hearing him swear softly, turned. Hutch came erect with a buckskin sack in his hand and he came back to Will. He untied the thong of the sack, then held out his palm and tipped the sack. A stream of bright eagles cascaded into his rough palm.

Hutch raised his glance to Will, then shuttled it to Cleff, and as if he could restrain himself no longer, he gave Cleff a savage kick in the thigh.

Will brushed him back, watching Cleff. The pain of the kick roused Cleff; he opened his eyes, and his glance, already black and hating, settled on Will. Slowly he pushed himself by his elbows to a sitting position and the two men looked at each other. There was an animal ferocity in Cleff's thin face, a will to kill in his eyes that went beyond any declaration in words. For the first time since Wilsey Kirk had brought the news of the massacre, Will felt a true raging anger.

Will said softly, "Let's start with Dickert, Cleff. You put a knife in him for what he had in his money belt, didn't you?"

Cleff didn't answer, he merely lifted a shoulder and wiped the blood from his cheek, his malevolent glance still on Will.

"Let's go to Keefe. You shot him and you ran off his horses."

Still watching Will, Richie Cleff spat in contempt. Hutch lunged for him, but Will barred his way.

Sudden shaking seized him; he did not know whether it was anger or fever that caused it, but he went on implacably, "Who was the third man, Cleff, the one who went south?"

"You'll see," Cleff said thinly. "Him and the others are likely only a couple of hours behind you."

Will's expression did not alter. If Cleff was afraid there was nothing in his face to show it, and in that moment Will knew that the man feared nothing. The thought of it was suddenly intolerable to him. Here was a butcher cornered at last, and his only answer to the charges against him was to spit contemptuously.

Will's shaking was almost uncontrollable now, its source a wild, almost heart-bursting anger. He looked at Hutch and said, "You think Cleff helped kill Mayze and the other three?"

Hutch only stared at him, as if not believing what he had heard. "Are you crazy, or am I? What's this?" He held up the sack of eagles.

"Then you're satisfied."

"I'm satisfied as hell," Hutch said irritably. "Come on. Let's tie him up and go."

Will looked about him, almost casually, and then his glance settled and he pointed. "We're going, all right. But just as far as that tree."

Hutch glanced in the direction Will was pointing, and when he saw the dead tree glistening with wetness, his glance whipped back to Will. There was shock in his eyes as he regarded Will. Hutch, Will saw, understood.

They were silent a long moment as if listening to the steady rain. Hutch licked his lips. "You sure, Will?" he asked hoarsely.

Will's voice was flat, final. "There's a hundred miles to travel and a dozen men to fight before a jury can decide the same thing we can decide here." He paused. "Go get his rope, Hutch."

Hutch's face seemed drained of all color, and he glanced fleetingly at Cleff. Will waited, and when Hutch made no move, Will said in a voice iron-hard with calculated cruelty, "You ran away from your wife, Hutch. You ran away from your job. But you're not going to run away from this."

It was as if Will had hit him. Hutch winced and for a moment there was hatred in the look he gave Will. Then, without speaking, he turned and tramped over to Cleff's downed horse. From the horn he untied the rope, but Will was not looking at him. Gun at his side, Will said to Cleff, "Get up."

Cleff didn't move.

Will took two steps toward him and held the gun six inches from Cleff's face.

"Maybe this way's easier," he said softly. "If it is, don't get up."

For the first time Will saw something like fear mingled with the wild hatred in Cleff's eyes. Cleff came slowly to his feet and Will stepped back on quivering legs. When Hutch came abreast of him he said, "Tie his hands behind his back. Not with the rope, with his saddle strings."

Hutch went back to the horse and presently returned with the leathers. Cleff made no move to fight and almost docilely submitted to Hutch's tying his wrists behind his back.

"Now walk over to that dead tree," Will said. With Will's gun in his back, Cleff stumbled the ten yards to the big pine. Hutch followed, and when they were under the biggest branch, Will said, "Stand right there." Then he glanced at Hutch. "All right."

Hutch would not look at him. He uncoiled the rope and threw the end over the tree branch, then tested it. The branch held his weight, and now, not looking at Will, he handed him the rope.

It was Will who slipped the noose over Cleff's head and tightened it.

Then Will moved around to face Cleff. "I'm sorry I can't do this twice," he said thinly.

Cleff spat in his face.

Slowly, Will wiped the spittle from his cheek and then he moved behind Cleff. He drew the slack in the rope and Hutch looked at him beseechingly. Will lifted his good hand and said, "High as you can reach, Hutch."

Hutch slowly, reluctantly, lifted his hands, then turned his back so that he would not see Cleff.

"Now!" Will said, and they both threw their weight onto the rope, falling to their knees against the weight on the other end.

7

They had their sleep out, which took them into the afternoon. When Will, propped against a tree, roused out of sleep there came that bridging moment when memory picks up the life that had gone on before sleep. With that memory now came an overwhelming depression, tinged with an indefinable feeling of guilt.

Fully awake, Will first noticed that Hutch's blankets had been added to his own that covered his body. A big fire was blazing in the misting rain. Hutch, seated with his back against a nearby tree, arms extended with elbows on knees, was staring morosely at the blaze as if hypnotized. Looking beyond the fire, Will saw a third horse picketed with their own. He knew that Hutch, waking earlier, had rounded up the breed's mount.

Not stirring, Will watched Hutch, remembering his reluctance to share in the hanging of Cleff. He recalled his own lashing fury that had crowded Hutch into joining him, and a deep shame touched him. Hutch had backed away from the hanging and Will did not even need to ask himself the reason. It was one thing to shoot and kill a man in anger or fear when you knew that the man would kill you if you didn't kill him. It was another thing to take a defenseless man with his hands tied behind his back and break his neck with a rope.

Will closed his eyes, but the image of Cleff swinging from the dead branch would not be shut out. It was a symbol, Will knew bitterly, of every fault—of overriding anger, of vengefulness, of merciless hatred, and of a savage will to punish.

He opened his eyes and surprised Hutch watching him. For an instant they regarded each other, and then Will saw Hutch's glance slide away. He found that he too felt a strange relief when he did not have to look in Hutch's eyes.

Hutch rose now, went over to the fire and knelt. When he rose he had a coffee pot, tin cup, and an ash-laden piece of pan bread in his hands. Coming over to Will, he halted, poured the coffee, and extended the cup.

"Where did we get this?" Will asked.

"In their outfit," Hutch said, not looking at him.

Will ate hungrily while Hutch rummaged around for sticks on which to prop the wet blankets facing the fire. Gingerly Will moved his left shoulder. Pain came immediately, and lingered long after he was quiet.

Hutch came over to him then and picked up the coffee pot and cup. "I found just as many eagles in Cardman's saddle bag as there were in Cleff's."

"That's two-thirds of it then," Will said.

For the first time now they looked at each other. "Will," Hutch said quietly, "let's get out of here."

Will felt a sudden relief, as if Hutch had put his own feelings into words.

They broke camp in silence, Will doing those chores which he could manage with one hand. The sleep, the warmth, and the food had restored a measure of his strength, but they had not restored his spirits. Once mounted, with Hutch ahead and leading the third horse, Will made an iron attempt to rationalize his feelings. True, he had ordered a man hanged, but the man was guilty of the blackest and most cowardly murders. He had received a rough justice where legal justice was unavailable. *But was it unavailable?* Will asked himself with bitter honesty. Couldn't they have taken Cleff back to Dry Creek, boarded a westbound stage, and delivered him along with the evidence to the nearest law officer west, all without Maydet's knowing that Cleff had been captured? Yes, they could have. Wasn't that why Hutch had been reluctant to share in Cleff's hanging?

Will looked about him through the slanting rain at the dripping trees and acknowledged that this was true. He could have delivered Cleff to certain justice. Instead, in his fury, he had elected himself witness, jury, judge, and executioner. Moreover, he had made Hutch an unwilling accessory. Strangely then, he thought of Carrie and of her answer when he had asked her, "How would you have me be?" *Gentler,* she had said. His answer to that had been this ultimate savagery, he thought dismally.

Sometime in late afternoon the rain slacked off and toward evening the sun broke out briefly, but the break in the weather saw no lift in the spirits of the two men. When full dark came, Hutch reined up and waited for Will to bring his horse alongside. It was as if it were easier for them to talk in the dark because they did not have to look at each other.

Hutch said, "Want to keep traveling?"

Will put off answering for so long that Hutch said, "Maybe you're tired."

"I'm like you, Hutch," Will said finally. "I want to put it as far behind me as I can. Let's keep going."

Alternately riding the third horse, they pushed on down the long canyon and sometime around midnight they halted to rest and give their horses the last of the grain. Hutch built up a fire and set the coffee pot on it while Will, his back and shoulder dully aching, rested against the tree. When they had finished the last of Hutch's biscuits and drunk their coffee, Hutch, squatting by the fire, looked across it at Will. It was the first time today that Hutch had really met Will's eyes.

"I wish we hadn't done it, Will," Hutch said quietly.

"You didn't do it, I did."

Hutch only shook his head. "I'm leaving Dry Creek, Will. I'm going back to my woman."

Will said nothing, only waited.

"I'm going to get so far from Maggie Boley I can't reach her." He grimaced and stared into the fire for a moment. "It took me a long time to grow up, but I made it."

Still Will said nothing.

Hutch continued to stare into the fire. Then, with an abrupt shift in thought, he asked, "Was Maydet the third man, Will?"

Will lifted his shoulder in a shrug that brought a nudge of pain to his back. He let it subside and then said, "I think he was, Hutch. That's too much money to risk losing by someone else's mistake."

"How much was it?"

"Sixty thousand dollars."

"Cardman had twenty and so did Cleff," Hutch said. "You think Lou Maydet ever split equal with his boys?"

"For this kind of money I think he'd be willing to," Will said thoughtfully. "First he had to get one man to kill each guard. These two men had to be willing to shoot down in cold blood men they knew and had probably worked with. Men like that aren't easy to find. Second, he had to get men who could keep their mouths shut, no matter what."

Hutch said wryly, "Cleff did."

Will nodded. "In other words, he had to get two men as tough as he was or it wasn't worth taking the risk. To get them he had to share with them." He paused. "I'm betting it was Maydet who killed Tim Mayze, Hutch. He knew Mayze and all the time he was division agent he was Tim's boss. I think he had to show Cleff and Cardman that he could kill a man he knew and probably liked and trusted and worked with. I think his promise to kill Tim was the only way he could get them."

"You think Cleff and Cardman were clearing out of the country for good?"

Will nodded.

"You think Maydet will?"

"No. I think he picked his men well." Will's voice was bitter. "Besides, we've killed all witnesses against him."

And that, Will was thinking, was another bitter reward of his hanging of Cleff. A few minutes of his wild and reckless anger had guaranteed Maydet immunity from punishment. There was not a man alive who could truthfully say that Maydet had a share in the robbery and killings.

Minutes later they had kicked out the fire and were riding again.

It was not yet dawn when they rode into the Dry Creek Station to be challenged by the alert stocktender. Will was bone weary and when the lantern was lighted Hutch had to help him dismount.

When Will was standing alone Hutch said, "Lay over a day and sleep, Will."

"I'll have to," Will conceded.

"Me, I'm changing horses and going home."

"I'll be by in a day or two. Pass the word about Cardman and Cleff."

Hutch hesitated and then said softly, so that the stocktender could not hear, "Nobody knows it, Will. They don't have to."

Will looked at him a long moment, then turned his head toward the stocktender who was rubbing down Will's horse with a grain sack. "You," he called. "Come here."

The boy came over and halted before them. "I'm going in and sleep," Will said. "When the eastbound comes through tell the driver that Hutch and I caught up with two of the robbers. Tell him Cardman was killed and that we hanged Cleff. We found the gold on them."

He turned to Hutch, whose face, in the light of the distant lantern, seemed drained of all protest, as if here was one more thing he must accept in payment for his dereliction.

"We take care of our own, Hutch. Let them know it," Will said quietly. He turned and headed toward the adobe.

* * *

Will spent the following day resting and sleeping. The morning after, he rode out toward the east, his destination Louisburg. Word of Cleff's hanging would have preceded him and he wondered if Maydet had the news yet. It seemed likely to him that Maydet, after the killings, would have swung south away from the immigrant trails where his sign would have been lost in the prairie grass. It would have been easy for him then to swing east, passing Louisburg to the south, and make his entry into Louisburg from the east. In the unlikely event of questioning, he would have a half-dozen of his men to back up his story that he was buying horses or feed. Will knew he wouldn't panic at news of Cardman's death and Cleff's hanging; he would only laugh, pleased that Midland had accommodated him by killing the only two men who could possibly testify against him.

Memory of that mistake galled Will, but not for that reason. He had taken a man's life as if he were a jungle enemy, setting himself above law and civilization. As the eastbound stage passed him, he realized that his act would give Midland the reputation for absolute implacability, which was necessary. But how much better it would have been if Midland had come before twelve men, asking only justice. Will could not bury the remorse he felt, and he knew only time could.

The heat of the day made the horizon shimmer, so that as he approached Lennor's the house and the new barn danced crazily in the undulated heat waves. Coming closer, he saw that Lennor had the walls of the new barn nearly raised and he put his horse over to the building.

Lennor was notching a log on the ground when Will reined in; the stocktender waiting to hoist the log spoke respectfully. Then Lennor, realizing someone was there, turned. In that instant of recognition, Will saw something very like fear come into Lennor's square face.

"It's coming along," Will observed.

"It's already too small," Lennor said, avoiding his eye. "I misfigured."

Will stepped carefully out of the saddle and the stocktender took his horse.

"Any news?" Will asked.

Lennor looked at him now, his eyes accusing. "No. You made the only recent news."

Will nodded, turned, and tramped toward the house. *I better get used to it,* he thought.

Crossing the road, he entered the common room. Mrs. Lennor was seated in the far corner sewing something that looked like curtains. She dipped her head in greeting and returned her attention to her sewing so swiftly that she did not see Will touch his hat brim. *That's two,* Will thought. *I wonder about Carrie.*

He went through the room and halted in the kitchen door. Carrie was at the kitchen table kneading bread, her arms powdered with flour clear to her elbows. She did not hear him and Will stood there regarding her. For a moment he had an unreasoning impulse to withdraw quietly, mount his horse, and ride on, rather than face the same thing in Carrie's eyes that had been in Lennor's.

Then Carrie, sensing another person in the room, turned. What Will saw in her face then was not fear; it was joy, and for a fleeting second Will thought her body on the verge of motion. The moment passed, and Will's gaunt beard-stubbled face altered faintly into a smile. "I didn't go to California, Carrie."

Now Carrie straightened and removed the flour from her hands by stroking her thighs. "I'd heard that," she said quietly. Whatever had been in her eyes was veiled again.

Will came slowly into the room. The question of what she had heard and, more important, what she thought of what she'd heard, was forming in his mind to be asked, but he checked himself. "How's Keefe?" he asked.

"Dickert asked him to come into Louisburg when he could travel. He left yesterday."

Her glance did not avoid his, and for this Will silently blessed her.

"How is your back?" Carrie asked.

"I'll have to have you tell me," Will said. He was watching her carefully, seeking for the least sign of uneasiness in her manner. All he could discover, however, was her usual matter-of-factness.

"The bunkhouse is empty," Carrie said. "I'll bring some warm water out and clean you up."

Will went through the kitchen and headed for the bunkhouse. Once there, he stripped to the waist and was clumsily untying the bandages when Carrie entered. Standing beside the table, Will was silent as Carrie, behind him, snipped off the bandages with scissors, gently bathed his back and side, then applied fresh bandages over the bear grease with which she covered his wound. On this bandaging she did not bind his arm to his side. When it was finished, Will shrugged into his shirt, watching Carrie tidy up.

Then Carrie did an odd thing. In the very act of wiping spilled water from the table top she looked abruptly at Will, dropped the cloth, turned away from the table, and slowly walked over to a bunk. She lowered herself to its edge and Will watched her, puzzled by her actions.

"I'm leaving the Lennors, Will."

Will frowned. "For where?"

"East or west, I guess it doesn't matter."

"Make it west, Carrie. You'll have a Midland pass to California."

A crease appeared between Carrie's dark eyebrows. "You really want me to go west, Will?"

"I only want to do something for you, Carrie. If you go west, I'll order out a messenger coach for you alone."

Carrie smiled fleetingly and Will was surprised to see color mount into her face. "I was thinking east, Will. There must be somebody there left that I know."

"Why are you leaving?" Will asked soberly.

"I'm not welcome here."

Will was silent for a moment. "Since taking me in?"

Carrie nodded and lifted her glance.

Watching her, Will said meagerly, "How did they take the news of Cleff's hanging?"

"Like I did. We hated it."

Will moved to the table and put a leg on it. Then he said slowly, "Would you believe me if I say now that I hate it, too?"

"But it's done," Carrie said quietly.

Will looked away, an intolerable sadness in him. He had cost Carrie all the small happiness she could gather to herself. He had placed her in a position where she could not refuse him help, but in helping him she had alienated all the meager affections the Lennors could spare her. He did not need to ask her how the Lennors had treated her, for he could imagine it. Needing her labor, yet wanting her to leave so that the risk of her friendship with Gannon would be removed, the Lennors were afraid to send her away. If they did, Gannon, the division superintendent, might retaliate. The only weapon left them was a chill sanctimoniousness, an unbending but never-expressed disapproval of Carrie which, as they knew it would, had now become intolerable.

Will said then, "Let me check the whole line, Carrie. There are good families running home stations. They'd welcome a girl who would work."

Carrie shook her head. "I want away from the line, Will."

"Because of me again?"

"Yes."

"Because of Cleff." It was a statement rather than a question.

"Yes," Carrie said again, "because of Cleff."

Will scrubbed his face with his hand and said presently, "God knows, I'm sorry for that."

"I'm sure you are, but that's not enough, Will," Carrie said tonelessly. "When you're crossed again, you'll do that or something worse. Each new thing is always worse than the last. It has to be or you can't keep people fearing you." He saw pity in her eyes, and he hated it more than ever. "Right now, Will, you're no better than a hired killer, hired by Midland. You didn't need to hang Richie Cleff. You just wanted to do something more terrible than they did to you. Using that logic, why won't you some day go quietly into Lou Maydet's room while he's sleeping and shoot him in the ear?"

"No, Carrie!" Will protested almost desperately. "No!"

He was thinking then of how he had stuck a gun in the sitting Cleff's face, saying, *Maybe this way's easier. If it is, don't get up.* What Carrie said was true, all of it.

"Or someone may kill you that way, Will. They hate you enough. Why should I stay and watch it happen?"

Will sighed, and rose. "You shouldn't, Carrie," he said quietly.

"When Maydet turned away from my door and you were lying unconscious under my bed, I owned part of you, Will, whether I wanted to or not. Now I want to leave before I have to watch you destroy yourself and my part of you, too."

"All right, Carrie," Will said. "Get away from the line. Go east. You haven't the money to do it though, have you?"

"No."

"You'll get it from Midland," Will said.

Carrie's face flushed. "I don't want to take help, Will, but I must. I can pay it back."

"Sure you can," Will said. "When are you leaving?"

Carrie rose. "Why not tomorrow? Why put it off?"

"I'll ride it with you, Carrie. We'll get you to the railhead and head you east."

Carrie smiled her thanks, moved over to the table, picked up her things, and went out. Tiredly Will moved over to the bunk and lay belly-down, feeling the clean luxury of his fresh bandages. Sadness was still in him and he wondered what his life on the line would be like once Carrie was gone. He recalled now her reason for going. She owned a part of him, she had said, and she did not want to wait and see him destroyed.

That could happen, Will conceded, but not if he could help it. He could and would ask the territories Midland passed through for law enforcement officers. If necessary he could ask that Midland's real property be assessed at a worth that would allow Midland to pay in taxes the equivalent of law officers' salaries. There had to be a way for the law to control and punish Maydet and remove that responsibility from Midland's hands. Why, he wondered bitterly, had it taken the loss of Carrie to make him face this?

The exhaustion of these past days overwhelmed him again and he slept.

That night after dinner when the stocktenders had left the kitchen, leaving Will and the Lennors still at table, Carrie broke her news. Standing between the Lennors' chairs, she looked down at Mr. Lennor. "I hope that was a good supper, Mr. Lennor," she said. "It's the last one I'll cook for you."

Lennor stared up at her with puzzlement in his square face, but Carrie did not keep him waiting. "I'm going east on tomorrow's stage."

"Using what for money?" Mrs. Lennor asked harshly.

"Using Midland money," Will put in quietly. "We owe her more than money."

Mrs. Lennor looked at him venomously and then

pointed out in her dry kindless voice, "You haven't any clothes, Carrie."

"I'm not naked. That's all that matters," Carrie said.

"This leaves us in quite a hole, Carrie," Lennor said heavily.

"A hole you dug for yourself," Carrie countered. "I don't think I've been a burden on you, Mr. Lennor. I've worked my way. You've both been kind to me and I'm grateful. I just think I should move on."

"Where will you go?"

"Any place where someone needs a hired girl."

Lennor looked at his wife as if asking for help. He wanted to protest, yet he also did not want Carrie to change her mind.

Mrs. Lennor settled it for him. "We'll miss you, Carrie, but neither of us would ever want to stand in your way."

"And I wouldn't want you to," Carrie said sweetly. She picked up a plate and turned away.

When the stage came in next morning, Will first learned from the express messenger that there was space in the coach. He arranged for Carrie's passage and loaded her valise in the rear boot. He purposely avoided the house and Carrie's good-bye to the Lennors. He watched the team change and the hub greasing and presently, at the driver's call, the passengers filed out, Carrie among them. She wore a pert straw hat, and her dress, which Will had never seen before, was of a dark blue material that made her chestnut hair seem even lighter. Both the Lennors came out on the porch and Carrie halted by Will, turning to wave to them for the last time. Four men stood aside, waiting for Carrie to step first into the coach.

"You don't mind riding alone, Carrie? I'll have to ride on top."

"Oh, your back," Carrie said. "I'd forgotten that. I'd better get used to riding alone."

After helping Carrie, Will swung up on the seat behind the box and the stage rolled out. Will kept remembering Carrie's last words and somehow the realization that they were true rankled in him. *If she has to travel alone, that's my fault,* he thought. For a brief moment Will wished bitterly that he had known Carrie some other time and place when his misjudgments and his mistakes would not have condemned him in her eyes. *I'm too late,* he thought with a grey wisdom. He had been too late in understanding Marian to keep her, and he had been too late in listening to Carrie.

Will's thoughts were interrupted by the driver's voice. "I hear Hutch is back at Helper Creek."

Gannon only nodded.

"They tell me you and him made a trip."

"So we did," Will said tonelessly, and looked at the driver. Something in his face held a warning, for the driver turned his head and spat and looked out over the prairie, once more minding his own business.

It was mid-afternoon when the log and sod shack of the Helper Creek Station appeared out of the prairie. As the coach approached, passing the house on its way to the corral, Will glanced at it. The door was shut and there was no sign of life.

The team change was ready at the corral and the reins were held by a man Will had never seen before. Where, Will wondered, was Hutch? He stepped down and was heading for the house when the stocktender called, "I wouldn't go up there, Mister."

Will halted and looked at the man, who obviously did not know who he was.

"Why not?" Will asked.

"They've had some trouble."

Will swiveled his head to look again at the house, and then, a rising alarm in him, he tramped across the hard-packed earth toward the house. His knock on the door went unanswered and he lifted the latch and stepped inside.

Seated at the table was Hutch's wife, and at Will's entrance she turned her head to look at him. Her eyes, once unreadable, were bright with a hatred that shocked Will. Then his glance shuttled to the bed in the corner. A blanket-wrapped figure, boots thrusting out, lay on the bed. Swiftly, Will strode across the room and lifted the blanket from the figure. It was Hutch, his face peaceful in death; the blood on his powder-burned shirt front had dried around the hole in his chest.

For stunned moments Will looked down at Hutch and then he gently replaced the blanket. He stood staring at the wall as if uncomprehending, an almost blinding surge of grief taking him. Then he turned and looked at Hutch's Indian wife. Slowly he crossed the room and halted beside the table. "What happened?"

Her fleshy face seemed to melt before his eyes; she covered her face with her hands, placed her head on the table and a wild uncontrollable sobbing seized her.

Will watched her a moment, then put a hand on her shoulder, pressing gently before he released her.

Turning, he moved toward the door, feeling a murdering anger rising in him. He tramped out to the coach, passed it, and hauled up before the stocktender.

"What happened? I'm Gannon, the super."

"I was sleeping in the barn when a shot woke me just before dawn. I heard a horse running, but couldn't see anything. I ran up to the house then and the woman started screaming." He paused. "I guess Hutch got up to answer the door for whoever shot him."

Will was aware suddenly that Carrie had come up beside him and now he turned to her. "You heard?"

Carrie only nodded; mercifully she did not look at Will. He turned and slowly walked over to the corral. There was no doubt in his mind now that Hutch's death was retaliation for his share in hanging Cleff. The only other persons who had reason for harming Hutch were the Boleys, and Will knew that Bales Boley was totally indifferent to his daughter's sluttish conduct. No, it had to be Maydet.

He halted at the corral and folded his arms on the top rail, looking at nothing, thinking of Hutch. In spite of his weaknesses Hutch had been a generous, warm-hearted friend and Will knew bleakly that he alone was responsible for Hutch's death. If he had not shamed Hutch into helping him hang Cleff, Hutch would be alive now.

"Will."

Gannon slowly turned his head to regard Carrie, standing beside him. There was that look of pity in her eyes that Will dreaded.

He said slowly, "Everything you said about me was right, Carrie. I'm to blame for Hutch's death."

Carrie said nothing.

"Even up till yesterday I thought I could back away from being Midland's hired killer." He paused. "Now I can't back away. Hutch was my friend. I'm going to bury him and then get Maydet."

"I know," Carrie said.

Will said slowly, bitterly, "You can't jump off a cliff, Carrie, then change your mind when you're about to land. I guess I've jumped." He straightened up and glanced back at the coach. The teams were ready and the driver was eyeing him impatiently. "Come along, Carrie," he said quietly.

She fell in beside him and when they reached the driver, Will halted.

"I'm staying here," Will told the express messenger. "Miss Bentall will go on with you. At Louisburg I want you to take Miss Bentall to Dickert. Tell him to turn over five hundred dollars to her, then have her escorted to the end of steel. Dickert is to pay her train fare to any place she names. He is to watch out for her at all times. Have you got that?"

The messenger nodded.

Will looked down at Carrie. "Anything you want, you ask for, Carrie."

Now he took off his hat, knowing this was good-bye, but not knowing what to say. He saw tears misting Carrie's eyes and he held out his hand.

Carrie ignored it. She came up to him, lifted her face, and kissed him, then said softly, "Take care, Will."

Blindly she walked past him and stepped into the coach.

Will stood rooted to the spot and watched the driver swing up and whip the teams into motion. He watched the coach until it was almost out of sight and he was thinking that it held all on this earth that was dear to him.

When he turned, he saw the stocktender watching him. "Get a shovel," Will said.

"I've already started it," the stocktender said. Together then they walked out a ways onto the prairie where fresh dirt mounded the grass. Alternately, Will and the stocktender dug Hutch's grave. Coatless, perspiration searing his wound, Will worked stubbornly, welcoming the pain that kept him from thinking. While Will spaded, the stocktender went over to hook up the teams for the westbound, and later, when the stage rolled in off the prairie to the east, Will paid it no attention.

The grave was shoulder-deep now, so that when Will heard someone say, "Mr. Gannon," he had to turn and look up.

Standing on the edge of the grave, his young face sober and controlled, was young Bert Dickert.

"What are you doing here, Bert?" Gannon asked.

"I'm hunting for you."

"Why?"

Dickert squatted on his heels and said quietly, "Maydet's crowd is expecting something. They've had watchers out since dawn. You ran down Cleff and I figured it might be you they were waiting for."

"It is," Will conceded.

"Then when the eastbound driver told me about Hutch, I was sure."

"Thanks for the warning, Bert. It's nice to know

I'm expected." His voice was thin. "They made sure I'd come, by killing Hutch."

"Well, two of us will be harder to get than one," Bert said.

"There'll only be one. You're staying here, Bert. If they'll kill Hutch, they'll kill you."

"You can't fight them all," Bert protested.

"I've been doing all right," Will said grimly, hating himself. "Let's finish this, Bert."

While young Dickert and the stocktender finished the grave, Will went up to the house to prepare Hutch's body for burial. Afterwards, with Hutch's wife watching stony-eyed, the child clinging to her skirt, they lowered Hutch's blanket-wrapped body into the grave. Bare-headed, they listened to young Bert Dickert say the prayer.

When the grave was covered over and Hutch's wife had returned to the house, Will asked the stocktender to saddle up a mount for him and get Hutch's saddle scabbard and rifle. Then he told Bert Dickert to talk with Hutch's wife the next day and reassure her as to the future. If she wished to stay here, the line would supply a stocktender and pay her a reasonable amount in lease money for her station. If she chose to leave, they would place her with some other station where she could work and provide for her family. Or, if she chose, they would pay for her passage back to Arizona and her people. The main thing, Will told him, was that she must know Midland would take care of her.

The stocktender returned with the horse and Will stepped into the saddle. "You'll hear from me," he told Dickert, and put his horse in motion, heading east for Louisburg.

He thought then of Carrie, alone in town. Unable to find Dickert, she would surely put up at the hotel to await his return. The irony of it did not escape him. Carrie was leaving the country so that she would not be a witness to future violence and death. Yet the very violence she feared would take place before she could leave.

It was night when Will approached Louisburg. The lamps were lighted in the shacks, the big store, and the hotel, making an island of light on the prairie's blackness. A couple of hundred yards from the edge of town Will reined up, dismounted, and drew Hutch's rifle from the saddle scabbard. He picketed his horse off the trail, then headed for town. His route was circumspect, swinging south of the town and coming into it at the rear of the hotel.

He stationed himself in its deep shadow where he could observe Maydet's store, the saloon, and the stables and corrals. The wide street held its usual quota of waiting stage passengers who walked aimlessly between the lighted buildings in search of some diversion. Will leaned the point of his shoulder against the building and watched the street, noting idly that there was a lighted lantern on a pole before the blacksmith's shop, as if some night repair had taken place or was about to.

He picked up, almost immediately, the pair of watchers against the saloon front. Looking carefully around the corner of the hotel, he saw a third man idling on its porch bench. Doubtless there was yet another man stationed around the corrals. Still Will waited, wanting to learn everything he needed to know before he moved.

Presently he saw a man come out of the darkness
from his side of the street and approach one of the
saloon watchers. Then the saloon watcher moved
away, going down the plank walk in front of
Maydet's store and continuing on toward the stable
area. He passed under the hanging lantern outside
the blacksmith shop and then moved into the dark
shop itself. Will's interest quickened. If the man was
on an errand or after some tool, why wouldn't he
show a light inside the dark building?

In a few moments the watcher emerged from the
blacksmith's shop, retraced his steps, and again took
up his vigil in front of the saloon. Now Will ignored
the watchers and concentrated his attention on the
blacksmith shop, whose double doors were open and
whose interior was unlighted. He could see no
movement around it.

He forced patience upon himself and presently he
was rewarded. From the direction of the stables he
saw a figure emerge into the circle of lantern light
and enter the shop. When the man made no effort to
strike a light and emerged almost immediately, Will
was sure the two watchers were almost certainly re-
porting to someone inside the blacksmith shop. Now
Will understood the reason for the hanging lantern.
Anyone riding into town might stop at the saloon or
store or hotel, but inevitably he must put up his
horse. To get to the corral he would have to pass in
front of the blacksmith shop. The hanging lantern
would light him while his ambusher would remain in
darkness.

Will quietly turned and walked to the rear of the
hotel. He moved past the dark shacks until he was at
the edge of town and then turned west. Keeping

wide of town he circled, crossed the trail, passed his picketed horse, and kept on north, coming into the town at the rear of Maydet's store. At its back corner he paused and waited again, listening for the movements of any watcher who might be staked out at the rear of the blacksmith's shop a hundred feet away. He saw nothing and heard nothing, and still he waited. Minutes later a third man passed down the street under the lamp and went into the blacksmith shop.

Will moved then, circling out into the deepest darkness, coming up at the rear of the shop. It was a log building, chinked with mud, and now Will leaned his rifle against a log and drew out his knife. Quietly he began to pry out a small section of the chinking, working slowly and taking infinite care to make no noise.

When the last section of chinking came freely, Will leaned down and peered through the slot left by the removed chinking. The interior of the blacksmith shop was dark but the lantern hanging on the pole in front of the shop cast a strong light on the ground under it. Silhouetted against this light Will saw two men seated in the shop, facing the lantern light, their backs to him. One man was hatless, but the swell of his massive shoulders told Will that Maydet himself was in charge of this ambush.

Will straightened, picked up his rifle, and moved along the wall, feeling its rough surface. All blacksmith shops he had ever seen had double doors, front and rear, wide enough to accommodate the biggest wagons. Presently his touch revealed lumber. Will moved slowly, feeling the door shape under his hand. He stopped where the two doors met and felt

for a hasp but did not find one. The fit of the doors
was tight enough that he could not get his fingers in
the crack.

Now he knelt, feeling the bottom of the door.
There were inches between it and the ground, and
he lifted and gently pulled one of the doors toward
him, testing it to see if it was locked. It kept coming
toward him with infinite slowness as he lifted its
weight; the rusty squeak of a hinge could betray
him.

When he judged the door open wide enough, he
rose, softly cocked his rifle, and slithered through
the opening of the dark shop. Both men were still
seated toward the front of the shop and they were
talking in low tones.

Will waited until they were silent and then he
called, "Here I am, Maydet."

Both men came to their feet; the man wearing the
hat shot immediately and Will heard the slug boom
into the logs ten feet away. The man shot again.
Now Will took careful aim at him and fired. Even as
he pulled the trigger he was moving to his left. He
saw the man go down, and on the heel of his own
shot Maydet fired. Will heard the slug racket into
the logs to his right.

Maydet must have heard the same sound of a
wasted bullet. He had had courage enough to wait to
get off his own shot, but when it failed him and he
knew it, he wheeled and broke for the door. Will
could see the gun in his fist, uptilted to wipe out the
lantern light. Will raised his rifle, lost its sight in the
blackness of Maydet's back and pulled the trigger.

Maydet never shot. He was already running, and
now, driven off balance by the impact of Will's bul-

let, he dived face-down on the hard-packed dirt. His gun tumbled out of his hands, somersaulted once, and came to rest.

Will moved swiftly out the rear door, pushed it shut, and traveled to the side of the building. Moving up along it, he waited in the darkness, reloading both rifle and pistol as he listened to the sound of booted feet running.

Two men appeared from the direction of the store at a dead run. But before they were well into the circle of lantern light a third man appeared from across the road. One man called and a fourth man, probably the stable watcher, answered. Then they were out of Will's sight; he moved swiftly toward the front of the building, his pistol drawn, his rifle cocked and held in his left hand. Rounding the corner of the building, he halted. One man was kneeling, rolling Maydet over on his back. The other three were watching, their backs to Will.

"Look this way, boys," Will called.

The three standing men wheeled almost in unison and the fourth man rose slowly. They were looking at Will's waist-high rifle leveled at them, and at the covering pistol in his right hand.

"Throw your guns on the ground. Do it slow, because I'm nervous," Will said meagerly.

With their boss dead, not one of the men was inviting a fight. Slowly the two men who held guns in their hands simply opened their fists. The other two slowly drew their guns from their holsters and dropped them.

Will said quietly, "One hour from now I'll cruise this town. If I see you, I'll shoot you. Now back off and get your horses."

The four men moved slowly out of the lantern light toward the corral, and Will lowered his guns. He looked about him and far out in the street he saw some idlers watching this, and then came the sound of someone running. Cautiously Will raised his rifle, backing toward the safe darkness of the blacksmith shop. Then a figure broke into the circle of lantern light and Will saw that it was Carrie. She came into his arms and he folded her to him, trying to still her shaking.

"There's no reason to leave now, Carrie. There's no reason to ever leave again."

She spoke into his shoulder, "I know."